THE LEGEND OF TITUS

T.S. MAYNARD

For my brother, a true legend

PROLOGUE

In 1215 of the year of our Lord, Charles Bedivere II conquered the whole of the Northern Territory after he defeated the triumvirate known as the three wicked barons. Charles became king, a position he could not have attained were it not for one man—Titus.

An unusual name for the land and no one knew his surname, but it didn't matter. Even a whisper of "Titus" filled allies with awe and enemies with fear. The soldier's bravery and ferocity were unrivaled, and he retired undefeated in battle.

As a reward for his service, King Charles offered Titus the role and title of chancellor, which would have made him the second most powerful individual in the region. In addition, the king presented the warrior with a vast swath of land and many peasants to work it. For reasons unknown, Titus refused. Rumors swirled about a fracture in their relationship as he was no longer seen in the king's court or anywhere near the castle. Instead, he became a mythical figure whose exploits were told in song and poem.

In reality, Titus settled on a small parcel deep in the woods beside a tranquil river, but the quiet waters did nothing for his tortured soul. The many years of fighting had taken a heavy toll. Debilitating depression over the war's cost had replaced his once youthful optimism. One day, on a chance encounter, he met a woman who would change his life.

Her name, Ariella, meant "lion of God," and although she carried no roar, she possessed a strength that calmed his anguish. She also introduced him to the Bible. The idea of a God who forgives all intrigued him, and he began to view Ariella as his angel sent from above. The two married, and in time, Ariella became pregnant. She gave birth to a healthy baby boy, whom they named Aidan. Titus lived a simple life tending to his crops and raising his son, but his past still gnawed at his conscience. His wife tried to persuade him to make amends with his old friend, Charles, but he brushed any suggestion aside, put his head down, and worked his field.

Ten years later, a plague ravaged the Northern and Southern Territories. The disease devastated the population until it finally took its last soul. Unfortunately, that soul was Ariella.

CHAPTER 1

One year later

"Why did Mom have to die?" Aidan asked his father as they both stood at the foot of her grave, which rested under a wilting poplar tree behind their homestead.

Titus's hazel eyes stared out into nothing, lost in thought. He stood almost six feet tall, and his shoulder length hair, once a deep chestnut, had dulled and now had streaks of gray. His calloused hands held a just bloomed wildflower, which he placed under a wooden cross at the head of the grave. Titus had crafted the religious symbol from beechwood, and despite a lot of effort, the two pieces of the cross were crooked.

"Why did Mom have to die?" Aidan asked again. The boy wore a simple deerskin tunic, and regardless of his father's bloodline, he would never be like him. Physically, he took after his mother. His hair was a soft brown, his eyes a bright green, and his frame slight.

"Only God knows," Titus whispered.

The youngster furrowed his brow at the unsatisfying answer.

Despite Titus's stoic and ethereal response, he often

wondered the same question when he was alone. His wife had taught him to read the Bible, and he couldn't reconcile how the loving God from the verses could allow those who followed to experience such pain. It left Titus believing he'd never been truly forgiven for the life he'd lived before as a warrior. His wife was an angel, so perhaps he was being punished. But why make his son suffer?

"I still miss her," Aidan said.

The words cut into Titus's soul. He didn't dare speak, or the flood of emotions bubbling beneath the surface would erupt. The old soldier had to remain strong for his thirteen-year-old boy, who believed he was already a man. Titus turned and walked to the field to resume working. It's how he dealt with all of his problems. Work. *Put your head down and grind away.*

Anniversaries usually commemorate joyful events, but not all of them do. After one year, the pain from Ariella's death ached just as much as the day she passed. When the insidious disease struck, Ariella isolated herself in the barn with the animals. She also refused to let Titus or Aidan near her, so all they could do was slide food and water under the door until the third day, when she no longer reached for it.

Titus tried to avoid such memories with labor—intense, back-breaking labor. He stabbed at the dirt with a dagger King Charles had given him. The blade was hand-crafted and made from the finest Damascus steel. The dagger's guard had diamonds etched into it, and tiny crosses decorated the grip. He twisted the knife in the soggy soil, creating a small divot six inches deep. Aidan followed behind, dragging a sack of seeds. He placed three seeds into the hole and then covered it with loose dirt. The plot of land wasn't huge, but seeding it still took several hours and there were sections for different crops—barley, wheat, oats, and beans.

Titus thrust the blade into the earth again and then stopped.

In one instant, his introspection switched off and his eyes narrowed. He stood and surveyed the forest like a deer scanning for predators.

"What is it?" Aidan asked.

"Someone's coming," Titus said.

His son looked around, confused. There was no sign of anyone. Seconds later, hooves pounded against the ground and echoed through the trees. Two men on horseback emerged on the trail leading to the homestead.

"Who are they?" Aidan asked.

"They're King Charles's men."

The first rider wore a crimson tunic with a silhouette of a lion's head emblazoned across the front in gold thread. He wasn't fitted for battle, but still wielded a massive broad sword that bounced on the side of his hip as he rode. His long gray beard hinted at his advanced age, especially when contrasted against his baby-faced companion, who had on a similar red tunic.

Both visitors pulled the reins of their horses and stopped a few yards short of Titus. The graying man dismounted and stepped in front of his horse. He smiled at Titus and gave him a big hug. "Titus. It is good to see you."

Titus remained guarded, but he couldn't stop a smirk from creeping across his face. "Harold. It's been a while. What brings you from the cushy court of the king's castle?"

"His death."

Titus's face dropped.

Harold shrugged. "Died in his sleep. The man survived battles, the plague, even his three wives, but a heavy nap finally got him."

Titus struggled to respond while processing the death of his once best friend.

Harold patted Titus on the shoulder. "The funeral will be in two days. He would've appreciated if you were there."

Titus dropped his gaze to the ground. It wasn't as simple of a request as it sounded.

"I understand if you need to think about it," Harold said. "I've got to deliver the message to other villages." He mounted his horse and guided the animal in the other direction. "It was good seeing you, old friend."

Titus remained in shock, both from the news and the implications of the king's death. "Harold?"

Harold turned around.

"Who will be the new king?" Titus asked.

"I don't know."

Both men shared the same concerned look. Titus caught Aidan staring at him, so he shook off the news and offered a polite bow to Harold. "Thank you for coming. I will... consider the request."

THAT NIGHT, Titus sat by the hearth, gazing at the dagger in the firelight. The crackling flames filled their modest one room home with a warm glow. He rubbed his fingers along the many crosses on the handle of the weapon as if pondering each one.

Aidan sat at their small table finishing a piece of bread while studying his father. "What do they mean?" He had asked before, but Ariella had always been there to change the subject. She had wanted her son to know who her father had become and not who he had been. Until now, Aidan had never been able to press the issue. "What do they mean?" he asked again.

Titus's finger stopped and his eyes flicked up. He turned and his gaze bore down on his son. *Should he tell him?*

Aidan pointed to the dagger. "The engravings. Tell me."

Titus flipped the blade, showing the hilt to his son, who approached for a closer look. "The diamonds represent the battles we won." Titus pointed to the dagger's guard.

Aidan counted the diamonds. "Ten. Did you ever lose?"

Titus shook his head.

Aidan raised an eyebrow, impressed. "What are the crosses? There are a lot more of those." Aidan ran his fingers across the tiny crosses that lined the handle, just as his father had done.

Titus considered his words. "Each one of those represents ten men."

"Were those soldiers under your command?"

"No." Titus pulled the dagger back and sheathed it. "This dagger was a gift from the king—a reward for my services." He paused as his thoughts transported him back in time. "I carry it as a reminder that God forgives all. At least, I hope so. One day, when you're a man, I'll give you this... because we all need forgiveness."

Aidan nodded with a perplexed expression and changed the subject. "Can I go with you to the castle? To the king's funeral?"

Titus offered a curt shake of the head, dismissing the notion.

Aidan pursed his lips. "Why not?"

"Because I'm not going."

"Wasn't the king your friend?"

"We *used* to be friends." Titus turned back to the fire and its dancing flames.

"Are you mad at him because he became king, and you didn't?"

Titus chuckled under his breath. "No. I didn't want to be king." He paused and reminisced. "Charles was supposed to be the king. He was very smart, and he had a grand vision of a land where everyone could work as they pleased. Everyone would have food to eat. Everyone would be safe and… happy." Titus smiled. "I wanted to live in that kingdom."

"Why didn't you remain friends?"

"It's complicated. And I wanted simple."

"Dad, I'd really like to see the castle."

"No."

Aidan's shoulders slumped, but he refused to give up. "We never go anywhere."

Titus snapped his neck around and stared at his son. "What happened when your mother left to go to the village?"

Aidan dropped his eyes to the floor, unable to speak of the events.

Titus didn't let that stop him. "She got sick. And she died."

"But the plague is gone," Aidan muttered.

"There's other evil in the world." Titus didn't revel in chastising his son, but he believed his primary duty was to keep him safe. "Get some rest. We have a lot of work in the morning."

Like every problem, work was the answer.

Aidan clenched his jaw but didn't protest further. He went to the small cot on the other side of the room, laid down, and faced the wall, away from his father.

Titus opened a small chest and removed a Bible with a leather binding. He flipped to a marked page where he'd last finished. It was Proverbs chapter 3. He began reading and the wrinkles on his forehead softened. Titus loved this time of day. It brought back memories of his wife teaching him to read. Whenever he cracked the Good Book open, he got butterflies as her soothing voice echoed in his mind or he'd reminisce about the many times she'd have to lean in and point to a word. Her sandy blonde hair would graze the side of his cheek. Titus would inhale and catch whiffs of sage from the soap she used.

Ariella and Titus had spent hours reading together and while he had an excellent memory and could quote verses from the Bible, he struggled to reconcile the different stories within it. Some passages even seemed to contradict one another. Exodus 21:24 preached an "eye for an eye" and Luke 6:29 proffered, "To one who strikes you on the cheek, offer the other also..." Titus chalked up his confusion to his limited education. He assumed smarter people understood the conflicting messages, and so he clung to the simpler story of the Gospel.

Titus's failure to understand the nuances of scripture and see the larger picture mirrored his past as a soldier. In the heat of battle, his movements were fluid, and he could recall training sessions with ease, but his understanding of battlefield tactics and war strategies eluded him. Those weaknesses were Charles's strengths, and the two balanced one another.

Charles.

Titus lowered the Bible as he remembered his friend. A twinge of regret crept in for not having reconciled with him. Maybe Titus should go to the king's funeral and pay his last respects. They had been a great team during the war. Other memories came to mind, causing Titus's face to stiffen. He resumed reading and put Charles out of his thoughts.

CHAPTER 2

The king's funeral came and went. Harold didn't return to inquire the reason Titus didn't attend, nor did anyone come to bring news of the next king. In fact, no one came for anything.

Titus and Aidan remained at the homestead and worked the land, but Aidan grew more and more restless. Even Titus's horse, Zephyr, seemed anxious for a ride somewhere new. The chocolate colored stallion whinnied and kicked at the barn door. Titus ignored both his son and steed. The angst would fade. It would just take time.

Spring drifted away, but Aidan's restlessness did not. When the boy plowed, he attacked the ground as if he hated it, and at night, he barely spoke to his father. Titus overlooked the fact that his boy was becoming a young man, and one day, he would leave home. But that day was still far off. At least, that's what Titus told himself.

More time passed and the swelter of summer arrived. The barley and wheat sprouted out of the coffee-colored soil in thin patches. Given Titus's below average farming skills, it wasn't a terrible start, and come harvest, it would be enough food to survive the winter.

After a day at the river, Titus walked back carrying two small fish. Aidan meandered behind him, carrying their two rods in one hand and a stick in the other. He pretended the stick was a sword and swiped at the grass as if battling an opponent, albeit a very short one. Neither spoke. Titus disappeared behind the house to clean the small meal while Aidan paced their field, searching for something to do.

The ground buzzed at first, but then it grew into a thundering quake as a dozen men on horses rode toward Titus's homestead.

With wide eyes, Aidan watched the men with delight. Each had a broadsword hitched to their hips, and they wore forest green tunics over black leather armor which, although cheaper than chain mail, appeared more impressive to the young teen. Muscles rippled across the arms of the men as they guided the reins of the horses.

Titus emerged from behind their home, hands covered in fish guts. As he walked closer, he studied the men, even though he had no desire to greet them. He didn't recognize the dragon crest emblazoned across the chest of their tunics.

The leader of this band, an overweight pot-bellied man with bulging arms and stocky legs, held up his hand for the entourage to stop. They obeyed and halted well short of the homestead to show respect.

Three other men stood out in this strange group. Two enormous ones, Enok and Gregori, rode on each side of the leader and served as personal guards. Of the two, Enok was the larger and more intimidating. The Bible describes the Nephilim as giants, and based on Enok's size, he could have easily been descended from them. His thick black beard covered most of the battle scars on his face, but a large one ran from the corner of his left eye to his chin. The facial hair refused to grow over the mangled line of flesh. Gregori only seemed small compared to his guard mate, but the man had a bear-like build. His powerful arms looked like they could carry the animal he rode on just as easily as it carried him. In contrast to the Herculean size of these two warriors, a clean shaven and scrawny man, Tooley, rode beside Gregori. His angular jaw-line and protruding cheek bones gave the impression of a skeleton covered in skin.

Out of habit, Titus couldn't help but evaluate how he'd fight if it came to that. Unfortunately, nothing about the situation favored him. He was old, outnumbered, without a sword, and there were two archers in back who rode out from the sides, giving a clear angle. At this range, he stood no chance. Titus took comfort in the fact that if these men had come to fight, he'd be dead already. "What can I do for you?" he asked.

"Address him as, my lord." Tooley pointed his sword at Titus.

The leader held up his hand for his subordinate to stand down. "My name is Marmaduke Rutherford the Third. I'm raising an army to bring the Northern and Southern Territories together at long last."

Titus gritted his teeth. These men had come to recruit an army. He should've seen it coming. It reminded him of Charles riding up to the village where he was born. He'd never been more than five miles outside of his home in the then seventeen years of his life when Charles rode in with his dazzling armor and charming smile. He spoke eloquently and forcefully about the tyranny of the three barons. The powerful words stirred something inside of Titus. Or perhaps he'd simply wanted to leave his small town. Maybe that's what Titus feared Aidan might do if given the chance.

He glanced at his son, who stared at the soldiers, mouth open in awe. These men would no doubt promise riches, a common tactic.

To ensure his message was heard, Marmaduke leaned forward. "I say again, I'm raising an army."

Titus shifted his attention to Marmaduke and offered a slight wave of dismissal to signal his lack of interest without being disrespectful. "We are but simple farmers," Titus bowed and side-eyed Tooley. "My lord. We wish you the best in your endeavors."

Marmaduke sized up Titus and found something intriguing, something he couldn't quite put his finger on. "Have you ever fought before?"

Titus hesitated too long.

Marmaduke smirked. "A man after my own heart."

"I've given that life up," Titus said.

Marmaduke chuckled. "Ah, come on." He dismounted and stepped in front of Titus. "You never really give it up, do you?"

Titus averted his gaze and stared at the ground. "Some do. I don't even have my armor or sword anymore."

Marmaduke studied Titus further. "That's rather foolish, don't you think?" He waved his hand toward the forest. "There's danger throughout these woods, whether from predators or thieves."

"I've put my faith in the Lord. He will protect us."

Marmaduke surveyed the simple home while standing beside Titus. "Is that so? What's that in your hem?" he asked without looking. He'd no doubt spotted the weapon as soon as he'd ridden up.

"This?" Titus withdrew the dagger, swung it around so the handle faced Marmaduke, and offered it to him. "It was a gift from King Charles. I use it…as a tool."

Marmaduke gripped the weapon. "You were with King Charles?"

"Many years ago."

Marmaduke assessed the dagger. "That's a lot of crosses."

He glanced at Titus with a hint of jealousy and skepticism. "I know what those mean."

Titus kept his eyes glued to the ground.

"What's your name?" Marmaduke asked.

Titus clenched his jaw and considered lying, but decided against it. "Titus."

Marmaduke raised an eyebrow and then turned to his men. "We are standing in the midst of a legend." He chuckled, which prompted his cronies to chortle in support. His eyes narrowed as he ran his fingers over the crosses. "Yes, I know what these mean. I also know how stories become exaggerated. A skirmish becomes a giant battle. An army of a hundred becomes an army of thousands. One kill becomes fifty. A soldier becomes a legendary warrior, yes?" He leaned toward Titus, who refused to make eye contact or respond.

"This would've made you a king." Marmaduke held up the dagger's handle as if it was damning proof of the statement before turning his attention to Titus's unimpressive farm. "And yet, here you are."

"Farming is harder than fighting," Titus said.

"I'm sure it is. Or maybe it's not suitable for your talents. I'm going to give you one more chance to join. There are a lot of riches to be made." Marmaduke half turned his head toward his men. "Isn't that right?"

The toadies laughed and huffed in agreement.

Marmaduke leaned in again and tried appealing to Titus as a father. "There's barely enough growing for the two of you. Think about your son. What happens when there's a drought or a poor harvest?"

Titus continued avoiding eye contact. "God will provide for us."

Marmaduke's cold eyes glared at Titus. Rejection in front of his men was never ideal. He tapped the blade of the dagger against his hand as he considered his response. "You seem to put all your trust in God. Are you sure that's wise? What has that gotten you?"

Titus didn't answer, but he knew these questions played with his son's mind, and maybe his own. He met Aidan's gaze, and in that moment, Titus could read his thoughts, because he'd been in the same position years ago and had the same desire to fight.

Marmaduke caught the two making eye contact and saw the opportunity. "And what about the world? The plague almost destroyed it. The king you served is dead and his kingdom has been in turmoil, as you surely know."

Titus racked his brain for something to say, but all he could muster was "Psalm 34:18."

Marmaduke sneered. "A Bible verse. That's your answer? Please share your wisdom, Titus." He waved his hand for Titus to speak as he walked in between him and his son.

Titus responded, "The Lord is near to the brokenhearted and saves the crushed in spirit."

Marmaduke ignored the words as if they'd never been spoken. Instead, he put his arm around Aidan. "What about you, young man? Are you interested in riches?"

"He's not." Titus raised his voice.

"Let the young man speak for himself, don't you think?" With his arm still draped over Aidan's shoulder, Marmaduke leaned down and pointed to the dagger's crosses. "You see these. Did you know that for everyone one, your father killed ten men?"

Aidan looked to his father for confirmation, but Titus stared at the ground.

"The king offered your father the position of chancellor. It was the opportunity of a lifetime, and he squandered it. Why shouldn't you get the same opportunity that he had?"

Titus faced his son. The boy's face flickered and grimaced with turmoil.

"And maybe your father can have another chance?" Marmaduke looked over at Titus.

The conflicted boy swallowed before speaking. "Um, I guess... I want to stay here."

Marmaduke dropped his head. It was not the answer he expected. He pursed his lips, took a deep breath, and then exhaled. "Very well. The legend of Titus is nothing more than a myth, anyway."

Titus ignored the insult and offered his son a subtle, proud grin, but Aidan didn't look at him. His eyes focused on something to Titus's left. A surge of terror filled Titus's stomach. He'd let his guard down and hadn't noticed that Enok now stood beside him.

Marmaduke plunged the dagger into Aidan's chest, and before Titus could react, Enok cracked him on the head with the butt of his sword. He fell to the ground, his world spinning.

Marmaduke tossed the blade into the field like it was junk. "You're too old, anyway, Titus. I need real men." He sauntered to his horse, mounted it, and rode away with the rest of his entourage.

Through bleary eyes, Titus crawled over to his son and cradled him. Aidan gasped for breath as blood gushed out of his chest. Titus held him with trembling hands. "You're okay, Son."

Aidan stared up at his father, fighting for life. With each strained exhale, a whisper of one word escaped his lips. "Why? Why? Why?"

Tears ran down Titus's cheeks as he tried to cover the wound with his hand to stop the bleeding.

"Why? Why?" Aidan's face became pale.

"You're okay, Son. It will be okay," Titus said.

"Why?"

Titus fought the flood of emotion and searched for an answer. "I don't know."

Aidan's gaze grew distant, and his body went limp. The boy had died.

CHAPTER 3

Blood oozed out of Titus's head from the pommel strike, but he didn't notice. He clutched Aidan's body and wailed in anguish. Never had he felt more alone or empty. The pain in his heart ached worse than any physical wound. A sword to the chest took a man out of his misery in seconds, but this agony served no purpose other than to torture without end.

Titus placed his son's body on the ground and ambled into his home, where he collapsed on the floor. Nothing mattered. There was no purpose anymore. He existed and yet he didn't. Or he didn't want to.

Night fell, and Titus remained catatonic on the floor. He'd neither eaten nor drank anything all day, but there was no hunger or thirst. Just a question and his son's final word.

Why?

Why had God allowed this to happen? First his wife and now his son. Why had God abandoned him? And why had Marmaduke let him live? He was who Marmaduke wanted in his army, not his son.

Why?

A howl of wolves jarred his senses. The animals were close.

The paws of the creatures pattered by the trees near the field. They'd come for Aidan's body. The smell of the boy's blood had lured them.

A rage and a purpose fueled Titus's soul. He sprang to his feet and ran outside. Three wolves circled the corpse with the largest, sniffing the bloody wound. Titus searched the ground for the dagger until he snatched it and charged toward the predators. He should have been terrified. Any of the three beasts could kill him. Somewhere deep in the recesses of his brain, he would've welcomed that outcome, but that wasn't his focus. These animals would face wrath in its rawest form.

The wolves growled as Titus approached, and the leader of the pack, a giant black alpha with blue eyes, stepped forward to guard his food and assert his dominance.

Titus pointed his dagger at the beast and crouched low, ready to battle.

The wolf snapped and snarled at the air, trying to intimidate Titus, who remained unbowed. The other wolves moved around Titus, encircling him and barking with an eager energy. They might have two meals, instead of one. The wolf on Titus's left, a mangy brown animal, jumped at Titus, with its jowls open wide. Titus sliced the dagger through the air, catching the animal's snout, causing it to squeal and retreat.

The distraction was all the black wolf needed. It leapt toward Titus, who whirled around and stabbed. The blade pierced the eye of the wolf and penetrated its brain. In one instant, the animal went from a ferocious beast to a lifeless corpse at Titus's feet. The remaining wolves paced side by side, confused without their leader. Titus charged, and the animals skittered into the forest.

Titus didn't celebrate the victory because there was none. There was only death. He stared at his son's body, then picked it up and carried it across the field where the boy's mother had been buried. Titus walked back to the barn, retrieved a spade, and returned to the gravesite. In the dead of night, he began shoveling. It was the closest thing to rest he would get because his tortured soul wouldn't permit sleep, and the digging allowed him to focus on the task at hand.

At least six feet.

No animal could disturb his son at that depth. Dirt flew to the sides.

Six feet.

The boy would be back with his mother. It was the only comforting thought Titus could muster. More dirt flew until an impressive pile built up beside the hole.

Six feet.

Titus dug until he stood in a pit taller than himself. He climbed out and brought his son's body down, careful to avoid looking at Aidan's face. It was too painful. He pulled himself out of the grave and pushed the mound of dirt into the hole. Filling the grave didn't take long, and within minutes, Titus stood at the foot, the deed completed. His eyes went from his wife's grave to his son's and then back. The only difference, aside from the freshly shoveled dirt, was the rickety cross at the head of Ariella's grave. Titus clenched the spade in his hand until a deep-seated rage erupted. With a powerful swipe of the shovel, Titus split the religious symbol into two pieces, but he wasn't finished. He swung again and broke the first piece, then the second. Swing. *Smash.* Swing. *Smash.* His tirade continued until there was nothing but splinters.

Winded and on the verge of tears, Titus dropped the tool and shuffled into his home. He collapsed onto his bed and laid there until fatigue forced his body and mind to shut down.

When morning broke, Titus's eyes cracked open, and for the briefest of moments, he felt normal, but that passed as soon as he recalled the day before. He laid in bed without blinking.

Why?

He still had no answer, but it didn't mean he had no response. Titus ambled outside to the corpse of the giant wolf. He picked up the dagger from the ground and stared at the blood-stained steel that had ended his son's life. His gaze shifted to the slain wolf at his feet. The animal had come to do evil. It needed to die. Marmaduke had come and done evil.

Titus resolved right then and there to thrust the dagger deep into Marmaduke's chest so he could watch the life fade from his body, just as he had to watch the life leave his son's. He drifted to the stable, mounted his horse, and left his home, never to return.

CHAPTER 4

Titus rode his aging stallion through the tall oaks and bushy pines. When he was younger, the chirping birds and swaying leaves in the wind would've brought a peace to his soul, but not today. All he saw was Marmaduke thrusting the dagger into his son's chest, and all he heard was his son asking that one-word unanswerable question. Nothing would take that away, but there could still be justice.

The horse carried him north. Titus assumed he'd eventually reach Fennelworth Castle, home of the royal court, a place he'd not been in over fifteen years. He didn't know who had been crowned king, or if he would be accepted, but he had no other choice.

Hours passed.

In his prime, Titus would've spied the men on horses hiding in the trees a quarter of a mile away. Maybe he did and just didn't care, but he offered no reaction until it was too late. Three horsemen sprang out to block his advance. Four more emerged behind, surrounding him.

"Who are you?" the bearded soldier closest to Titus asked.

He held a giant, shimmering sword and wore polished chain mail.

Titus didn't respond.

"Who are you, man?" The soldier pointed the blade at Titus to show the stakes.

With empty eyes, Titus stared back.

The soldier shook his head. "Last chance." He spurred his horse forward and reared his weapon back.

"I come to fight for King Charles," Titus said.

The soldier halted. "King Charles is dead."

"I come to fight for his replacement."

The soldier gave Titus a once over and sneered in disapproval while dismissing any notion he could fight. The old man before him wore no armor, carried no shield, and didn't even possess a sword.

From deep within the trees, another horse galloped up. "Let him through," the rider said. It was Harold.

The soldier guided his horse back several steps.

"It's lucky I came," Harold said to the soldier. "Or you'd be dead."

The soldier watched with a skeptical gaze as Titus rode past to Harold.

"I'm surprised to see you," Harold said to Titus. "Where is your boy?"

Titus didn't respond. Harold didn't need to ask anything else, and he didn't press for details. "The world is cruel sometimes."

Titus changed the subject. "Who is king?"

"Kensington."

Titus stopped his horse until Harold turned around to receive a scolding glare. "Kensington?"

Harold exhaled and puffed out his cheeks. "He's not the same boy you remember."

"That's good, because the boy I remember was more enamored with his looks than fighting. He weaseled out of the fiercest battles, but he always celebrated the victories."

Harold shrugged and deadpanned, "Yes, but he was very handsome doing it."

TITUS AND HAROLD left their horses in the stable, and four guards escorted them through the halls of Fennelworth Castle. Decked out in crimson tunics with the lion's crest, they carried short spears, whose tips glistened in the flames from the sconces on the stone walls.

They entered the king's salon, where a group of nobles argued and pointed to maps and scrolls splayed out on a massive oak table.

The loudest of the bunch shouted, "The Duke of Cheshire will provide ten knights for ten thousand acres."

"Ten thousand?" A noble held his head in shock. "That's robbery."

The reporting aristocrat tried to defend the proposal. "His knights are fully equipped and they might take some of the less desirable acreage in the east."

"Duke of Gundry offers thirty archers for 1,000 silver," another aristocrat said.

"That's not a bad price."

"For the next ten years," he added.

The nobles guffawed at such a ludicrous offer.

At the center of the bedlam was a man with flowing locks of auburn hair, a manicured beard, and a velvet burgundy robe. The epitome of majestic elegance, the striking individual explained how commoners would believe that God ordained people to rule. How else could such beauty be explained? This

24

was King Kensington, and after a few months of trying to fill the shoes of the prior king, he already showed the first signs of stress from the job as a deep wrinkle had formed just above his perfect eyebrows.

"Any offers from Lord Chaucer or Lord Gilroy?" Kensington asked.

A few nobles shook their heads. Kensington grunted with irritation. Chaucer and Gilroy were the two most influential lords who had yet to declare a side.

Raising an army was not a simple task. It required an extraordinary amount of logistical support, favors, and, most of all, money. Knights and mercenaries could be hired for a price, but they didn't come cheap. And then there was the equipment. Premium black smiths were needed to make swords and armor. Tailors, seamstresses, and shoemakers were employed for the uniforms and footwear.

Every man did not receive equal treatment when it came to expensive fittings. Those with limited fighting capabilities were expected to bring their own weapons and shoes. They would be given a basic crimson tunic to avoid confusion on the battlefield, but that was it. The allocation of resources made it easy to differentiate between trained nobles and common foot soldiers. Men on horses, protected by armor and wielding a steel sword, were dangerous *and* wealthy. Everyone else was disposable, even if they didn't know it.

The one exception to the rule—archers. Ambitious elites placed considerable value on men skilled with a bow, as they could change the entire course of a battle. Depending on their deployment, archers could disrupt lines of cavalry or decimate infantry ranks. They weren't as expensive as knights, but they weren't cheap, either.

The court of nobles presented various proposals from dukes and barons, all of whom looked to capitalize on the war. It was likely they'd sent offers to both sides. The trick for them was to pick the victor while getting the most out of the deal. A king or would-be-king had the challenge of avoiding mortgaging the entire kingdom before winning it. Hence the chaos.

The cacophony of yelling and debating proposals resumed until Kensington raised his hand for silence. He noticed Titus standing in the doorway. None of his court recognized the disheveled old man. "I'd like the room," he said in a booming voice.

All but one noble gathered their scrolls. The lone holdout, a haughty wiry man, raised his pleading hands. "We need to sort out these offers. We need—"

Kensington held his hand in front of the noble's face, which silenced him. He and the other men ushered themselves out.

Harold patted Titus on the back and followed the nobles.

The guards closed the door, leaving Titus and Kensington alone.

"It's been many years, Titus." Kensington approached and scrutinized his appearance. The clothing and unkempt hair were the polar opposite of Kensington's.

"Indeed it has."

"Why have you come?" Kensington asked.

"I come to fight for you."

Kensington raised an eyebrow. "Fight for me? I thought you hated me."

"Hate is a strong word. I simply didn't like you," Titus said.

Kensington chuckled. "You were always honest. That I could count on."

"Then you know that if I give my word to fight for you, I will."

"Why?" Kensington asked.

There was that question again. *Why?* Titus had an answer to this one, but he wasn't prepared to share it. "I have my reasons."

"Hmm." Kensington stroked his beard. "But are your reasons aligned with mine?"

"Do you want to win and defeat Marmaduke?" Titus asked.

Kensington studied Titus for a long moment. "Do you swear to obey my orders?"

"Let me know how I can prove it… my lord." Titus added the last part as a gesture. He never would've uttered those words in the past.

Kensington smirked.

CHAPTER 5

A page, no older than sixteen, escorted Titus to the armory, where a large wooden door and a well-armed guard protected the storeroom of war. "I have orders from Lord Kensington to fit this man with armor and a sword," the page said.

The guard opened the door, revealing a room twice as big as the king's salon, with three rows of shelves. The first contained armor for the legs, chest, arms, and head. Metal and wooden shields lined the second, and the last row held over a hundred steel swords, each crafted by the king's personal black smith.

A man's sword said something about him. It showed his fighting style, his strength, and often revealed his wealth. Individuals wielded the short sword and arming sword with one hand. Two-handers included the bastard, long, and great swords. Aside from the length of the blade, the variations consisted of width at the base, sharpness of the point, and size of the grip.

Titus shook his head in disbelief as he stared at the ostentatious display. Most of the pieces incorporated unnecessary designs and accessories. One of the great swords, a behemoth of glinting steel, contained sparkling carnelian and topaz in the hilt. One could have crafted two short swords from the amount of metal in the single blade. The gems adorning the sword could have been sold to purchase another three. It was everything Titus hated about the royal system distilled into a single item. He considered leaving, but Kensington walked up behind him and patted him on the shoulder. "You need to look the part."

"Can I at least pick my sword?"

"No," Kensington said without hesitation. "I remember that embarrassment of a short sword you used to wield. It barely had a guard on the hilt, and the leather around the handle was cracked and falling apart."

"Yes, but it was effective."

Kensington eyed Titus to remind him of his word.

Titus bowed in deference. If Kensington needed to pick his sword, then so be it, and of course, Kensington reached for the gaudy, thick great sword with the jeweled hilt. The heavy, garish weapon felt awkward in Titus's hands as he spun it. It also clashed with the rest of his appearance. "Now I can fight?"

Kensington shook his head. "No. You also need to visit my servants for a grooming."

Titus began to doubt his decision to return to the castle.

———

TWO HOURS LATER, Titus stepped out into the bailey of the castle in glistening armor, new leather shoes, and his massive sword sheathed on his hip. A trimmed beard and coifed hair had replaced the shaggy, unkempt appearance. Titus looked regal, but he felt ridiculous as he paced over to the other soldiers. Those dressed like him leaned against the back wall in the shade while two practiced dueling in the center. The commoners sat along the opposite wall in the sun. Those with energy playfully knocked their wooden swords against each other. Archers honed their skills on the far side of the open grass area, shooting arrows into bales of hay. Shouts erupted for an amazing shot and jeers after an embarrassing one.

Several men side-eyed Titus. The old man was unknown to this generation of warrior, at least in person. In the stories, he was seven feet tall, covered with muscles, and possessed a smile that could disarm any maiden.

Titus continued past the curious stares and assessed the men. Even within the noble ranks of warriors, there was a hierarchy. Those with all the accouterments of war grouped themselves on the right, and those with leather armor and no shield were on the left. Titus went to the left. He took up a spot beside a small man with craggy leather and a short sword. The man's eyes widened with surprise and he stepped backward to yield his position to Titus.

"Hello, sir," Titus said.

"Hello, sire." The young man's voice squeaked. He couldn't have been a day over nineteen.

"What's your name?" Titus offered his hand.

"Walter. From the House of Sharboord." He shook Titus's hand.

The elite warriors gave a slight disapproving glare, but remained focused on the duel in front of them. The practice duel was a simple concept, something Titus liked, but it wasn't realistic, something he didn't. Whoever scored three points first, won. This contest was already two to nothing, with the advantage to the larger soldier. As the fight proceeded into the third round, the larger noble stepped back in a feigned defensive maneuver. His opponent fell for the trap and attacked. The larger man spun the great sword around, cracked the opponent's weapon down, and snapped his blade up into the side of the man's armor. Point and match. The nobles applauded. Both warriors bowed toward each other in a show of respect, but the winner's grin and haughty walk to the sideline revealed his arrogance.

The custom of such duels was to challenge someone of a similar rank. Titus didn't adhere to such conventions and walked out into the area of battle, and pointed at the biggest man among the noble elites.

"You. Shall we go?"

The giant man, Knut of Cumberland, stood six and a half feet and weighed as much as an ox. His broad shoulders and thick arms made his great sword appear smaller than Titus's, even though the blades were the same size. Knut smirked. "Are you sure that's wise?"

"Why wouldn't it be?" Titus asked.

"Well, kind sir, I don't believe we've had the pleasure of meeting, but I dare say that I'm in the prime of my days, and you are… in your years of wisdom."

Quiet snickers arose from the elites.

"Then perhaps my wisdom can teach you how to lose gracefully."

Uncontrolled chuckles and chortles caused others to take notice.

"Don't say I didn't warn you, old man." Knut stepped into the grass and as the two men squared off, the size difference became more apparent. Titus gave up six inches and fifty pounds to Knut, and the great sword twirled like a toy in the big man's beefy fingers. He charged Titus, who held up his blade and absorbed the first mighty strike, but it sent him stumbling backward. Knut pressed forward and swung again. Titus deflected the steel with his weapon, but lost his balance, allowing Knut to swing from the other side. The massive blade cracked against Titus's armor. Point Knut.

The crowd laughed and jeered.

Kensington emerged from the castle's keep and stood at the edge of the line, watching from afar with curiosity.

Panting, Titus squared off for round two. This time, Titus went on the offensive and swung over the top. Knut blocked the attack as he backed up, and when the blades locked, he planted a boot in Titus's midsection, sending him sprawling on the ground. When Titus attempted to stand, Knut already had his blade pressed against the armor on his chest. Second point, Knut.

The nobles cheered even louder, while Kensington stroked his beard with concern.

"I suppose I'll have to learn how to *win* gracefully on my own." Knut smirked and then added insult to injury. "Finished being embarrassed, old man?" He didn't wait for a response, assuming the match was over. Knut moseyed back to the others.

Titus pulled himself to his feet and walked to Walter. "May I borrow your sword, kind sir?"

Confused, Walter handed over his short sword.

Titus leaned his giant weapon against the wall and returned to the dueling stage. "Excuse me, sir," Titus called to Knut. "Unless I'm mistaken, it's best to three."

Knut raised an eyebrow and chuckled. "Okay, old man. Let's get it over with."

"One more," Titus said, with the short sword in his left hand.

Knut rose and snorted, offended that he was being called out again. He faced Titus and charged like a bull. Titus sidestepped and reared the sword around and connected with the back of Knut's armor. The nobles gasped and howled at the unexpected turn of events. A point for the old man, and with a dinky short sword, no less. Knut laughed it off as well. His jaw tightened and his eyes narrowed. No more games. He turned and faced off, ready for a proper duel.

The men circled each other. Knut held his giant blade up in the high guard position, while Titus kept his short sword at chest level. Knut feigned right and then struck down to the left. Titus stepped from side to side and deflected the momentum of the giant blade, never absorbing it. His graceful movements were lightning quick as if he knew what Knut was going to do before he did it. The giant soldier bristled and swung with all his might. Titus jumped back, avoided the strike, spun, and swung, connecting with the armor on the giant soldier's midsection. Another point. The men let out a collective howl of approval, which infuriated Knut.

Kensington studied the reaction from the nobles and smirked.

"One more," Knut said.

Titus nodded, and the men squared off for the final deciding point. The blades clashed again and again, but Titus kept his poise. Knut's swings lost their pace, and his eyes no longer carried the same conviction. With his energy fading, he grunted and swung with all his might. Titus blocked the blade just in time, but the blow knocked Titus off balance. Knut seized the advantage and charged to finish the duel. He swung again, but Titus rolled forward, avoided the slash, and finished with his sword pointed at the big man's stomach. If this were a battle, Knut would be dead. Armor couldn't stop a blade from piercing through the metal.

The on-lookers clapped and cheered in shock.

Knut gritted his teeth, then bowed, accepting the defeat.

Titus remained kneeling. With his head lowered, he played it off as if he was being deferential even though he'd won, but the truth was he'd wrenched his back when he rolled over. His knees also ached. He stood and kept a stoic face, despite the pain. Titus never revealed weakness to anyone, or himself, for that matter, but as the nervous spike of energy faded, the throbbing intensified. He should've known better. It had been years since he last fought. Titus ambled back to the lower noble and was about to return the sword, but Kensington stepped over.

"You may choose your own sword," Kensington said, and then walked away.

Titus cracked a smile. At least something good came out of his injury. He pointed to the beat-up weapon, then to Walter. "Would you be open to a trade, kind sir?"

Walter's eyes lit up as he held his beautiful and expensive new sword. "Thank you. What's your name?"

"Titus."

Both the nobles and common soldiers within earshot fell silent.

CHAPTER 6

The elite nobles whispered among themselves while gawking at Titus, who stood beside Walter. Across the bailey, the common soldiers pointed and gossiped. The chatter spread to the archers, who lowered their bows and stared.

Walter swallowed and considered leaving, but the giant sword in his hands gave him confidence to open his mouth. "Titus, as in, the Titus from the war against the barons?"

Titus lowered his gaze and offered one small nod.

Walter made eye contact with the other nobles, who pointed to Titus and gestured for him to come over. "They want you."

Titus glanced in their direction, but didn't move. He raised his voice so anyone could hear. "Don't whisper like little children. If you have something to say, come here and say it."

Everyone converged around Titus. One of the common soldiers mustered the courage to speak first. "Did you really kill a hundred men at the Battle of Gundel?"

"I'm unsure of the number, but the battle was very bloody."

An archer shouted from the back, "Are you immortal?"

Titus chuckled, which elicited laughter from everyone

around him. "No. I can assure you I'm not, and as you can see, I'm getting on in age."

One of the best dressed and equipped nobles asked, "Why did you refuse to be the king's chancellor?"

The wrinkles on Titus's forehead deepened as he considered his answer. "I'm not much for administrative positions."

A commoner half-raised his hand. Titus nodded for him to speak. "Are we going to win this war?"

A noble laughed. "Of course we are. We have Titus."

The group cheered in support, but the gesture didn't move Titus. They gawked with wide-eyed wonder, but many of them would not survive. Some would die because they didn't know how to fight. Others would die randomly from an arrow they never saw coming.

"There's no guarantee of winning anything," Titus said. "Battle isn't like these practices." He waved his hand toward the bailey and the training taking place. "Most of the time, you're not fighting one on one. That idea sounds nice and honorable, but it isn't reality. When the fighting begins, there aren't rules or points. There's just death. Start training like you want to live."

The convicting words left most men silent.

Knut waved people back to their designated places. "Alright, enough talk. Resume training."

The men dispersed and separated themselves by class. Once Knut had the knights together, he waved two men to the center. "No more points. First to score, wins."

While the subpar training resumed, Titus remained next to Walter, who asked one more question, "Are you really going to fight with us?"

"Why else would I be here?" Titus spotted Harold across the bailey, leaning out from a large window in the stable, taking it all in. "Excuse me, Walter."

Titus ambled across the grass and did a double take when he caught sight of the castle's chapel in the corner. Underneath the chapel was the kings' crypt, where Charles had joined the last five kings in their eternal rest. Titus had almost forgotten this had been Charles's castle for over a decade. He brushed it aside and continued on until he reached Harold. The two nodded toward each other, and Titus leaned along the railing of the stable next to his friend.

"No pretend fighting for you?" Titus asked.

Harold smirked. "I'm too old. I'll save it for the battlefield."

"So you hang out with the horses all day, huh?" Titus chuckled as he waved his hand toward the animals behind.

"Well, I am the king's marshall."

"Really?"

The king's marshall was a high-ranking position within the court, responsible for the royal stable and who also assisted in managing the army.

"I'd rather deal with horses than nobles," Harold said.

"Very true."

"So, what do you think?" Harold motioned to the soldiers.

Titus looked over at the bunch. "They don't get it."

"You thought your little speech would change that?"

Titus shook his head. "I guess a battle is something you have to experience."

Both men remained quiet as they relived past horrors. Titus glanced again at the chapel and remembered the bloody battles with Charles. Clanging swords snapped Titus from his daze.

Knut dueled another knight with ferocity and anger, still insulted at having lost to Titus. "What's his story?"

"That's Knut of Cumberland, but his family isn't from Cumberland. They came from a land far to the east. His father was a Duke."

"A Duke? What happened?"

"His father backed the wrong noble in a war, so they had to flee. King Charles gave him a manor house in Cumberland and a baronet title, but the proud man never used the title because he hated it so much. He died a couple of years ago and Knut's been full of piss and vinegar ever since. He's determined to restore his family's honor. Your good friend, Kensington, promised a better title after the war."

"Fighting for titles. Always admirable," Titus deadpanned. His gaze turned again to the chapel.

"If you want to go into the crypt, I could ask Kensington. I'm sure he'd allow it."

"No."

"Then why do you keep staring over there?" Harold titled his chin toward the chapel.

"You know who else is buried with Charles?"

Harold didn't answer the rhetorical question. Everyone knew who was buried in the crypt.

"Baron John, a man I cut down." Titus tapped his chest. "That bastard raped women and murdered innocent men while he was on the throne, and yet, Charles demanded that we treat his body with respect. What about all the people who died for Charles? Or even for John? Did they receive the same 'respect'?"

Harold shrugged. "Like it or not, Baron John was the king, even if only for a short while. It's the custom to bury him in the king's crypt."

"Yeah, well, follow the customs and nothing changes."

"Is that why you disappeared?" Harold asked.

"Why did Charles say I left?"

"He said some men are built for war and nothing else."

Titus huffed. "Maybe so, but here's what's gonna happen, Harold. We're going to win Kensington some battles. He'll be thrilled. He might even throw us a party, but then, something is going to change. He's going to believe it was because of *his* leadership and strategy. He'll be so full of confidence in himself that he's going to engage the enemy in the final battle. And when that battle occurs, there will be a point where it could go either way. In that moment, Kensington will realize he's not in control of anything. He's going to be scared, and he's going to look to us to bail him out. When we do, there will be another party, and then he's going to tell himself that *he* did it. And not only that, he deserved it."

"So, *nothing* will ever change then?" Harold asked, disappointed with Titus's cynicism.

"One thing will be different this time. Marmaduke will not be buried in that crypt or any other. That I can promise you." Titus walked off toward the water barrel for a drink.

Kensington's steward ran up alongside him. "King Kensington would like a word with you."

"Tell the king I'm training." Titus kept walking. He had no interest in talking anymore.

The steward hurried to keep pace. "It's about your son."

Titus stopped in his tracks.

TITUS ENTERED the king's salon as Kensington ate a venison steak while evaluating maps and proposals for mercenaries and equipment. The steward closed the thick doors, leaving the two men alone.

"I'm glad to see you still have your fighting verve." Kensington dabbed his face with a napkin, a new item of the time reserved for the wealthy elites.

Titus had no interest in small talk. "How did you know about my son?"

Kensington leaned back in his chair. "I'm the king. It's my job to know things."

Titus eyed him, demanding more than a trite answer.

"Marmaduke has killed other family members after someone refused to join him. Word has spread, something he knew would happen. It wasn't hard to put the pieces together."

The reminder of Aidan's death created knots in Titus's stomach.

Kensington rose to his feet and paced across the room to the large window with his hands held behind him. "Titus, imagine for a moment that you've heard these stories. Marmaduke rides into your village, but instead of this evil monster, he's charming and kind. Rather than a threat, he offers you more money than you've earned in years. Are you going to say no, risk your life and the lives of your loved ones?" Kensington shrugged at his own query. He turned and faced Titus. "Why would he kill your son and let you live?"

The words left Titus silent as he'd racked his brain over that very question.

"Do you think perhaps he wants you to fight...and die? Imagine if the legendary Titus stormed the battlefield in anger, only to be felled by the first hail of arrows. His men would be emboldened. My army would be demoralized."

Titus shook his head. "One soldier can't affect a battle that much."

"What happened in the bailey?" Kensington asked. "As soon as the men heard you were among them, how did they react?"

Titus couldn't spin the truth, so he didn't respond.

Kensington stepped toward Titus. "The little things can matter, Titus. You just don't know which ones it will be. I'm not taking a chance that this is one."

Titus's eyes flared and his voice raised. "You're not going to let me fight? Then why did you let me join?"

"You are still known, and you are still respected. That much is obvious. A war involves more than fighting. I need you to help convince people to join *my* army."

Titus clenched his fists and kept them balled behind his back. It was all he could do to keep the rage from boiling over. "I'm not a recruiter. I must fight."

"You gave me your word, Titus."

"To fight for you!"

"You will fight, Titus." Kensington leaned toward Titus and locked eyes with him. "Now you have *my* word. You will fight. But only when the time is right. Do we have an understanding?"

Titus seethed with frustration. This type of gamesmanship was why he hated being around the castle and the nobles.

"Do we have an understanding?" Kensington asked again.

Titus knew that if he had any chance of killing Marmaduke, he'd have to play by Kensington's rules. For now, at least. He nodded.

"Good. Go get me more soldiers."

CHAPTER 7

"Marmaduke is the fourth wicked baron," Knut said, surrounded by a small crowd of men, women, and children dressed in modest animal clothing. Decked out in full fighting regalia, Knut wore the standard crimson tunic embroidered with a lion's head. It covered polished armor that gave the illusion he was even bigger than his already massive frame. "He brings death to our land."

One child glanced back at the nine knights dressed similarly to Knut. They sat atop hulking stallions in a perfect line, with Titus in the center. His horse was a young chestnut stallion in its prime, rather than his old steed, and had a frilled crimson banner that draped off its midsection.

As the designated leader, Knut held the king's standard, which billowed in the light breeze. He gestured to Titus with his free hand. "And who has heard of Titus?"

All heads turned to gawk at the living legend. Two fathers leaned down to their sons and pointed for them to get a good look at the mythical figure.

Knut continued with his pitch. "Titus rose to the challenge

and stopped the tyranny. It is time for the next generation to take up arms beside him and answer the call."

Titus stared ahead with dead eyes. Fortunately, no one could tell the difference from a stoic gaze. This was the tenth recruiting trip he'd been on over the last four weeks and he'd hated them all, but he'd kept his word to Kensington. The entire time, he thought of his son and the vow he'd made to avenge his murder. Having dueling promises tugged at his conscience, but never tore it, as the two weren't in direct conflict, at least not yet. One would simply have to wait.

But when would the armies collide? That question weighed on everyone. Though it was a simple query, it didn't have a simple answer. The season for war began after the spring planting and finished before the harvest. The limited campaigning period was a function of logistics, food, and survival. If the farmers couldn't plant and harvest, then there'd be little to no food and *everyone* would starve. Because of this inconvenient truth, farmers serving in the army would return to their fields when the leaves changed, and only the mercenaries and knights would remain together over winter.

With fall coming any day, soldier and commoner alike assumed the battle to decide the crown would take place the following year as neither Marmaduke nor Kensington seemed willing to risk everything on an incomplete and green army. Instead, they focused their energies on expanding their forces, which was the purpose of these village visits. Titus was brought for the spectacle, but Knut delivered the request.

"To defeat the invading force commanded by the evil Marmaduke," Knut said, "King Kensington needs an extra ration from the upcoming harvest and four men to serve in his noble army."

The energy and faces of the villagers dropped. Of the twenty-three people, only six men were of fighting age. Little did they know that the goal of each trip was to enlist at least fifteen able-bodied men. Knut had already reduced the requirement given the village's population, and he generously allowed for two men to remain to protect the women and help with the manual labor.

"Decide who will serve, and we will return in three days." Knut bowed in a show of respect, mounted his horse and led the convoy out of the village.

The knights traveled along the main trail that ran the length of the Northern and Southern Territories. No stone had ever been laid, so the rough path couldn't be called a road. The barren strip existed because of the volume of man and beast that had trampled across it through the years.

Sir Portnoy, a rotund knight, assessed their direction with concern. "We're traveling south."

"Yes," Knut answered.

"But that was the last village in the swamplands," Portnoy said, his voice uneasy.

"Kensington has ordered us to recruit no less than fifteen men."

Portnoy shifted in his saddle. "But the next villages are near the Valdik River."

Knut didn't bother confirming the statement, but his silence left the group on edge. The Valdik River was the unofficial dividing line between the two territories. Even though neither army had engaged in a full scale battle, smaller units had fought in three skirmishes. The minor and rare clashes occurred when recruiting parties crossed paths. Titus hadn't been involved in any of the three, which had resulted in eight casualties for Marmaduke and five for Kensington. Despite the minimal losses, the deaths reminded everyone of the stakes.

Kensington initially ordered recruiting trips around the heart of the Northern Territory, but once the largest villages had been visited, they had to expand the area. This trip would be their first to the Valdik, whereas Marmaduke's forces had already crossed it several times.

The knights rode along the path without speaking, and though unusual for them, it was typical for Titus. Most days, they joked and spoke with confidence, maybe even arrogance, and they carried themselves with a bravado as if they were invincible. As they swayed atop their horses, a somber reality set in. Death didn't care about any of that, something Titus knew all too well. He'd lost many friends during the war with the barons. Those painful memories were the reason he didn't talk much or bond with the men. During meals, he either sat by himself or he talked to Harold. At night, he laid in a tent outside the castle's walls with the other common soldiers, but he didn't share one. He rationalized that if he avoided getting close to anyone, then it wouldn't hurt as much when they died. It also allowed him to remain focused on his goal—killing Marmaduke.

The journey to the Valdik took another hour, but finally, the cavalcade reached the first hamlet which contained a half dozen hovels constructed with stacked logs. Hardened mud plugged the spaces in between. The women sat together beside the homes, grinding flour and cutting vegetables, with the children tucked close. The men labored in the fields, pulling weeds among the unripe oats.

Knut lifted the standard high as they entered the village. "Vassals of King Charles, gather round." Knut waved people over with his free hand.

The men kept their heads buried in their work as if no one had spoken.

Knut raised his voice. "I say, vassals of King Charles, gather around."

The farmers toiled away faster and moved further into the

field. Except for an occasional furtive glance, the women and children also acted as though the knights weren't there.

Knut guided his horse closer and waved for the other soldiers to follow. "King Kensington sends his greetings to you. As loyal subjects, he needs men to serve in his noble army to fight the evil Marmaduke."

Something stirred in the trees past the farmers. Then, a rustling of leaves and neighing of horses came from behind the knights. Titus swiveled his neck, and a jolt of fear shot through his veins. They were going to be attacked from two directions. "Prepare for battle!"

CHAPTER 8

Knut unsheathed his sword and reared his horse backward, a difficult maneuver with both hands occupied, one from his weapon, and the other from the standard. His eyes darted back and forth, searching for danger.

"Drop the flag and prepare to fight," Titus said.

Knut glanced at the flagpole in his hand, then at Titus. *Was he serious?* Protecting the flag was an honor and not something taken lightly.

"Do you want to live or die because of a piece of cloth?" Titus asked.

Knut tossed the pole to the ground.

"Form a line," Titus commanded. The soldiers surrounding Titus obeyed.

Within seconds, horsemen wearing Marmaduke's signature green tunic and black leather armor emerged from the trees past the fleeing farmers.

"What now?" Knut asked.

"We attack before they flank us. Forward!" Titus pointed his sword at the enemy, while urging his horse and the others to increase their speed.

The foe in front hadn't tightened their line yet and the attackers from behind revealed themselves, only to be surprised that their opponents were already gone.

Titus and his men stampeded across the farm as the villagers scrambled out of harm's way. Tooley, Marmaduke's skinny toady, commanded the unit. His eyes widened with panic from the fury charging at him. "Fall back to the trees," he ordered.

If Titus led the knights into the forest, their line would be broken and it was possible Tooley had traps or other men waiting. "Hold." Titus held up his hand and pulled the reins of his horse to stop the charge. The horses panted from the run and the men sucked wind from the fear.

Exposed in the center of the field, Titus jerked the reins and forced his horse around. The enemy behind had formed its line. Eight knights. Titus already counted the ones in the trees. Eight there as well.

"What do we do, Titus?" Knut asked. "Do we retreat that way?" He pointed to the thick trees behind the hovels.

"The people would be at risk," Titus said.

"What about that way?" Knut gestured the opposite direction.

Titus shook his head. The river down the hill would leave them pinned. He also had no interest in retreat. "They want us to split up or force us to the river."

"So what do we do?" a young knight asked, his voice cracking.

Titus pointed to the enemy line. "Knut, lead the charge. Stay tight. Do not break! As soon as we pass, everyone makes a hard turn to the left." Titus maneuvered his horse, so he was on the left edge of the formation.

Knut guided his stallion in the middle. "Forward," he commanded.

"Tighter," Titus called out.

The animals pinched in as they barreled toward the eight horses riding toward them. Tooley emerged from the trees behind and reformed his line. He ordered a charge for a rear attack.

At the moment, Titus and his men had a slight numerical advantage, but that would change as soon as the enemy lines converged. The same thought must've run through Knut and the other knights' minds. *How could they fight from both directions?*

"Faster and tighter," Titus commanded.

The men obeyed out of fear.

The two sides barreled toward one another on a collision course with only thirty yards separating them. As the distance closed, the details of the enemy became clearer. The opposing faces were just as scared, maybe more so, because the knight in charge reared to the side, causing the line to split, half to the right and half to the left.

Titus sliced his blade through the air as they passed and hacked off the arm of an enemy. The man shrieked in horror, but the thundering hooves muted the sound.

"Hard left," Titus shouted. He yanked his reins and pulled his steed around and drove his heels into its sides. The animal sped toward the four foes that had splintered off. The enemy knights were about to turn, but when one man looked back, his eyes bulged. Titus and the others were right behind them and closing. The split force changed direction again, but their retreat led them into Tooley's charging line. As the melee of horses passed one another, Titus yanked hard on his reins again. "Hard left."

They now pursued Tooley's disrupted line. By the time Tooley realized what was happening, it was too late. Titus and his men were upon them. As Tooley guided his forces around, blades swung from behind and four enemy knights toppled to the ground, dead.

"Retreat!" Tooley shouted.

Marmaduke's men charged away, eager to flee the battlefield.

Titus reared his horse in all directions, searching for anyone else to fight. The other men caught their breath and stared in awe as the legendary warrior paced his stallion around the village. His rage and nervous energy would've continued, but it stopped when a red tunic among the bodies captured his attention. The soldier lay on his back, eyes open and legs twisted in unnatural positions. It was Sir Portnoy. Titus only knew his name, but the death still sickened him. Titus guided his horse to the fallen man, dismounted, and knelt beside the body. The lifeless eyes stared past Titus into nothing.

There were no visible wounds and Titus could only assume Sir Portnoy had toppled off and either been trampled or he'd broken his neck. Titus heaved the body over his shoulders and placed it on the haunches of his horse. He mounted his stallion and guided it out of the village.

———

AFTER A VICTORY, it was customary to ride in a procession formation with chants or songs that let everyone know the good news, but the knights rode into Fennelworth Castle in a haphazard manner. Knut had retrieved the standard and held it high. Three other men trailed behind him, carrying the weapons of the dead enemy soldiers.

The archers and soldiers in the bailey would've cheered for such a sight were it not for Titus and the other three knights plodding behind with somber faces. A hush fell when people noticed Portnoy's body on the back of Titus's horse.

Harold emerged from the stable and walked over to Titus. "What happened?"

"We were ambushed," Titus said.

"But we killed five," Knut added.

"We lost Sir Portnoy," Titus said.

"Five?" an archer asked in disbelief.

"Huzzah!" another soldier shouted and raised his sword.

Others joined in and cheered. "Huzzah! Huzzah! Huzzah!"

King Kensington hurried into the bailey and was briefed by a noble. He held up his hands for quiet and then bellowed so all could hear. "Today is a great day." He motioned to the knights. "Our fearless warriors have defeated evil because God wills it! Tonight, we celebrate their victory!" He clapped at two stewards. "Bring out ale and bread."

Boisterous cheers erupted.

Titus eyed Harold with an "I told you so" look as he climbed off his horse and waved over a squire. "Make sure Sir Portnoy's body is properly tended to." He handed the squire the horse's reins.

"You alright?" Harold asked.

"Of course," Titus said in a wooden tone. "Let's celebrate before the final battle."

"You don't know that's what Kensington will do."

Titus didn't bother arguing and retreated to the dining hall to drink alone.

THE FESTIVITIES BEGAN IN EARNEST, with men indulging in alcohol and singing songs. Throughout it all, Titus moved from one place to the next, drinking by himself. He found a darkened corner inside the castle, a quiet spot along the castle's wall, and finally, the stable where he passed out.

Late the following morning, a steward discovered him and reported his whereabouts to the king, who came out alone and nudged him with his foot. Titus stirred and then held his throbbing head while collecting his senses.

"I'd been looking for you all night," Kensington said. "I'd seen neither hide nor hair of you."

"Fancy that," Titus said.

"I wanted to congratulate you on the victory," Kensington said.

Titus lifted himself off the ground and stood, his feet wobbly. "One of the men died. He would not consider it a victory."

"That happens in war. They tried to ambush you, Titus. Let's count our blessings."

"We were lucky. The men aren't ready. They don't understand battlefield tactics."

"Five of the enemy are dead. It appears they understand something."

"We were lucky," Titus repeated.

"Well, Marmaduke's luck has run out. We will engage with his army. We will win, and we will end this." Kensington held up his fist and clenched it as if squeezing Marmaduke like a bug.

Titus's jaw tightened. It was just as he'd predicted. He kept his head low for fear he'd say something he couldn't take back.

The lack of enthusiasm confused Kensington, who exhaled with frustration. "I thought you, of all people, would be pleased. You were so eager to fight before."

Kensington was right. Titus should've been giddy at the opportunity for revenge, but he wasn't. He kicked at the ground. "To fight, you need to be willing to die." Titus looked up and made direct eye contact with Kensington. "Are you?"

His question was more of an accusation, which was not lost

on Kensington. "I know you think very little of me, Titus. You may not recognize the value I provide, but each man has his skill. Mine is to lead."

"From safely in back, no doubt."

Kensington bristled. "I could have you arrested for such a comment."

Titus locked eyes with Kensington, daring him to follow through on the threat. But Kensington needed Titus, and he'd never arrest "the legend" before the battle to decide the crown.

Kensington softened his tone. "If no one leads, others don't know what to do. Is it heroic if I die leading a charge and then even more men die?"

Titus glared at Kensington with disdain. He didn't see a king. All he saw was an opportunist, but he would not win this argument with personal attacks. "A battle is nothing to be rushed into."

"We are prepared, Titus. We have the best equipment and the most men. And besides, we have you. Still undefeated in battle." Kensington tried to lighten the mood with a wry grin. He reached out his hand to pat Titus's shoulder, but after noticing the daggers in his eyes, he opted against it, and returned to the castle.

Titus leaned against the stable wall and slouched back down to the ground. He remained dazed as the reality of war set in.

The rest of the afternoon soldiers and squires ran around the bailey, preparing packs and going to the armory to have their weapons sharpened or shields fixed. Mobilizing an army took at least a day, which left Titus plenty of time to think, but that ended when Harold entered the stable to prep the horses. As soon as Harold saw Titus, he looked away.

"Do you believe me now?" Titus asked.

"You don't know what's going to happen, Titus."

"It would appear that I do."

Harold pulled a saddle off the wall. "There was going to be a battle at some point. We all knew it. And he's not wrong to fight."

"You think the men are ready?"

"As ready as they'll ever be. If we wait for spring, there's a chance Marmaduke gains the support of Lord Chaucer or Lord Gilroy. He also might hire mercenaries from foreign lands. We have the advantage right now. It's what Charles would've done."

"Hmm," Titus said in a half grunt.

"This is why you came, isn't it? To fight."

Titus refused to answer the question and asked his own. "And what happens after the battle?"

"Why do you care? You're going to leave again."

The dig got under Titus's skin. "You're right." He got to his feet and walked past his old friend. "Let's go to war."

CHAPTER 9

Kensington ordered the men to march the next day. Most celebrated the news because they believed they'd have a quick victory, which would mean they'd be home soon, but the mood changed when fatigue from the trek set in and a scout returned with an update.

"My lord," the scout said, "Marmaduke's army is heading north."

Kensington smiled. "Marmaduke is even more desperate than I thought."

Harold shifted in his saddle and nudged his horse toward the king. "How do you figure?"

"He was just defeated by my forces. No doubt that demoralized his men. He's worried his troops will desert over winter, so he's looking to engage beforehand."

Titus listened nearby and took the news with suspicion. Before most clashes, one army endeavored to evade the other, so the attackers attempted to corner the retreating soldiers into an advantageous battlefield while the fleeing side tried to trick their opponent to a location of their choosing. In this case, both sides were prepared to engage.

As was the custom, emissaries exchanged messages asking the other to surrender. When both rejected the offers, the armies agreed to battle beside the small town of Kent. Within two hours, the sides faced one another across a large meadow that stretched east and west. Bushy trees lined the edges, which made retreat difficult. Fleeing forces would either become splintered amongst the timbers, or they'd stay together in a direct line while the opposition attacked from behind.

Such a pitch favored the larger army—Kensington's, in this case. He commanded two thousand men—fifteen hundred infantry, two hundred and fifty archers, and a similar number of mounted knights.

Marmaduke's forces comprised thirteen hundred men—a thousand infantry, two hundred knights, and a hundred archers. Only a handful of knights had metal armor. Everyone else wore thick black leather.

A cool breeze whipped across the field, causing the grass to bend to one side. On any other day it might've been refreshing, but for every man on that pitch, noble or commoner, it chilled them to the bone despite their best efforts to present brave and intimidating faces. Today very well might be the day they died, and if it was, it would be gruesome. A sword might be thrust through their belly. An axe might smash their skull, or an arrow might rip through their flesh. Some type of injury was almost a certainty and the bigger the wound, the greater the likelihood of an infection afterward.

Two standards with the king's crest billowed in the light wind behind the army, where Kensington sat atop his majestic white stallion. In front of him, the infantry soldiers huddled tight for tactical reasons and out of fear. Their lines were one hundred wide and ten deep. There wasn't room on the flanks to go wider without blocking the cavalry. Armed with short swords and wooden shields, the men stood silently or whispered prayers.

The cavalry glistened in their polished armor while the protective masks hid their emotions, but they were no different from the infantry. Despite the difference in class, death was life's great equalizer. Every man must face it.

Positioning men was a critical component of battlefield tactics and often determined the victor. Both sides had a plan for how the initial forces would engage and an expectation of how the battle would progress. One side would inevitably be wrong. Savvy leaders could alter strategies in the heat of combat, and they did so with reserve detachments positioned behind the primary units.

Marmaduke placed his archers on the north end of the field, infantry in the center, and a cavalry contingent on the south. It was a basic formation with no units held in reserve.

Kensington had the numerical advantage in every category, so creating a counter configuration was simple. He matched Marmaduke's positioning, with a few key differences. First, he put half his archers on the north side of the field and the other half on the south. This gave his men the ability to rain missiles from two directions, which would demoralize the infantry and disrupt their lines more than Marmaduke's archers. Kensington also held a reserve detachment of fifty knights with himself and two other generals. These soldiers would rush to the aid of any struggling unit. Titus had been placed in this group.

Despite his undefeated record, Titus had never been in a battle where he felt confident, and he looked down upon any man who pretended otherwise. His jaw clenched while he tried to find the flaw in their formation, but Kensington had his men positioned properly and the army appeared pristine in their crimson tunics. There was nothing left to do, except what Titus had always done—win. He gripped the handle on the dagger in the sheath tied around his armor while he glared across the field at Marmaduke. Today, revenge would be his.

"Infantry forward," Kensington shouted. The soldiers planted their right feet and then banged on their shield on the left step. The cadence continued with booming thuds every other step to intimidate the opposition, who also began their march toward the middle of the battlefield.

Little did Marmaduke know that Kensington had laid a trap. After the twenty-fifth boom, the men stopped pacing, but maintained the rhythmic banging. The enemy kept closing the distance. Kensington smiled. His troops remained out of range of the opposing archers, but Marmaduke's men were now exposed.

"Archers," Kensington shouted. "Fire at will."

The archers aimed their bows to the sky, drew back an arrow, and then released. The arrows let out a high, almost inaudible "pfft" as they sailed into the air. Marmaduke's infantry stepped together, dropped to a knee, and raised their massive shields to create a protective wall. As the arrows rained down, the soldiers shrieked and howled.

Kensington nodded in approval and waved for the archers to continue firing. Titus maneuvered his horse to the side so he could have a better look. The cries were intense, but there was no break in the shield wall.

"Knights, full speed," Kensington said. "Infantry, resume march."

The knights charged forward in five rows of twenty horses. They raced along the northern and southern tree lines while the infantry surged. The goal was to annihilate the enemy archers on the north while the infantry charged the men hunkered on the battlefield. Once the two infantries were engaged, the southern cavalries would clash. After the northern knights destroyed the archers, they would flank the southern enemy knights. If the infantry or knights needed help, Titus and his men would ride to their aid. The battle would be over in minutes, but something grabbed Titus's attention—movement in the northern trees. A crossbowman hid behind a thick trunk. And there were others!

"Stop!" he shouted to the charging knights, but it was too late.

Kensington caught sight of it too, and his face dropped as he realized what could happen.

Titus dug his heels into the sides of his horse and galloped away at a breakneck speed.

"Titus, retake your position," Kensington said, but it was no use. Titus was like a bull seeing red. He charged as fast as his animal would carry him and closed the gap.

Marmaduke's archers took aim at the knights, who held up shields. Their horses had armor on their muzzles, chests, and flanks. It would require a precise shot to take down either man or beast, but some would be hit. Every clash was a numbers game. Who could incur the fewest losses and disrupt their opponent's lines enough to force a retreat?

A dozen crossbowmen stepped out from the trees and also took aim. The knights couldn't defend arrows coming from two different angles, and the power of a crossbow at close range could pierce their armor. A barrage of bolts sailed through the air, and over half of the first line of knights fell to the ground in a heap. Their horses drifted out of formation, causing the lines behind to break to avoid them.

This left a remnant of the first line charging the archers. With a hundred bows aimed at a handful of knights, they didn't stand a chance.

Making matters worse, a second row of crossbowmen stepped out from the trees to target the next wave of knights while the first group reloaded.

The strategic disadvantage of a crossbow was the time to reset the device. For maximum power, it could take as long as thirty seconds. Kensington's knights attempted to rally during the reprieve, tightening their formation, but the barrage of bolts from the second line of crossbows struck and stopped their momentum. Several men collapsed and a few horses reared in pain, further disrupting the charge.

A third line of crossbowman emerged and targeted the remaining knights. The bolts zinged through the air, delivering more death and carnage.

Titus guided his horse on the edge of the trees to avoid the melee of horses. The first group of crossbowman had almost reloaded, but it proved too long for the enemy closest to Titus. His head tumbled to the dirt after one swing of Titus's sword. The old warrior didn't stop and barreled forward through the second foe.

Another crossbowman had reloaded and took aim at Titus. The bolt zipped through the air and tagged Titus's horse square in the chest. The animal collapsed, sending Titus crashing to the ground. Running high on emotion, he ignored any pain, sprang to his feet, and hacked an arm off the man closest to him. A scared crossbowman tried to crank the bow faster. His fingers fumbled, but it wouldn't have mattered. Titus's sword pierced his midsection, and he fell to the ground.

Titus fought on through the trees, a one-man army, but the main battle had turned. Kensington's southern contingent also faced crossbowmen and met the same fate as the northern unit. This swung the numerical advantage in knights in Marmaduke's favor, which left the infantry exposed.

Titus fought on and felled a dozen more men until an archer took aim and launched an arrow that struck his right shoulder and knocked him to the ground. Given the short distance, the force of the arrow pierced Titus's armor and wedged deep in his flesh. The blow and injury left him writhing in the dirt, eyes blurry. In the fog of battle, Titus witnessed Marmaduke's forces encircling the infantry until many of Kensington's soldiers panicked and fled. Enok, Marmaduke's gargantuan henchman, rode through the ranks of fleeing men, cutting them down with swipe after swipe of his massive war sword. The power and ferocity reminded Titus of himself when he was younger, except Enok was bigger and more terrifying.

Titus had only seconds to escape. Once Kensington's forces withdrew, the enemy would search fallen soldiers for valuables and kill anyone still alive. He pulled himself to his feet and stumbled through the trees. A crossbowman aimed from twenty yards away. Titus moved behind a tree as the bolt whipped through the air, grazed the trunk and wedged in the side of his right thigh. He tried to run, but the searing pain left him dizzy. All Titus could manage was a plodding hobble while another crossbowman took aim. Titus glanced back at the soldier who would end the legend. The slight man had been scared to death a moment earlier, but now he sneered, knowing there was nothing left to fear.

CHAPTER 10

A knight broke through the tree line behind the crossbowman and ended him with one swipe of his massive sword.

Titus leaned against a tree trunk, stunned, as he watched his savior guide his horse over. It was Harold.

"Come on!" Harold held out his arm.

Titus grabbed it with his uninjured one. Harold hoisted him onto the back of the horse. The maneuver knocked both of the arrows wedged in Titus's body, causing him to bellow in pain.

Across the battlefield, Marmaduke studied the battle's progress like a hawk. He pointed in Titus's direction. His giant henchman, Gregori, and two other knights obeyed the order and barreled toward Harold and Titus.

With only one arm, Titus struggled to hold on while Harold steered the horse deeper into the dense forest. They would not escape with speed.

Marmaduke's men closed in, but as the trees got thicker, they had to slow down and traverse through the timbers.

Harold spurred his stallion while branches lashed across his helmet. Titus wrapped his left arm around Harold's midsection to avoid being knocked off.

A streak of light pierced through the leaves. Harold led the horse to it and the duo emerged on the edge of a steep hill. "Hold on," Harold said as he urged the horse down.

The scared animal whinnied and snorted as it stumbled down the slope.

Titus almost fell off several times, but he wedged his fingers under Harold's armor and steadied himself. When they reached the bottom, Titus noticed a ravine that split through the forest. Before he could muster a word, Harold had already led the stallion in that direction. The crevice had no trees, which allowed them to ride at a faster clip. Titus glanced over his shoulder. Thankfully, no one pursued.

The ravine became shallower until it melted into the rest of the woodlands. The panting steed begged for rest, so Harold slowed their pace and guided them into the thickest grouping of tree branches. The horse snorted and neighed with relief.

"Shhhh." Harold patted the animal on its neck and hoped it would understand the mortal danger if it didn't obey.

Titus leaned against the back of Harold, almost unconscious from the pain.

The horse and the forest settled into an uncomfortable stillness. Harold continued rubbing the horse's fur to keep him calm. *Had they escaped?*

A twig snapped and then leaves crunched. Marmaduke's henchmen had not given up. Their horses continued stepping through the undergrowth, the crunching getting louder and louder.

A voice shouted, "It's over. Accept your fate like a man."

Both Titus and Harold remained silent like ghosts rather than fighting a lost cause and becoming ones.

"Come out and we will spare your lives," Gregori tempted in a loud baritone voice. "Bow down to a real king. Otherwise, we will hunt you and every last man and kill you all."

Silence.

"Cowards," Gregori shouted.

Neither Harold nor Titus were dumb enough to move a muscle. They waited several minutes until the sound of hooves drifted away. They erred on the side of caution and extended their wait until Titus's pain reached an unbearable level, causing him to groan.

"Hang in there, Titus."

Titus groaned louder. Harold led the horse out of the thicket and down a dry creek bed. The two rode for another hour until they arrived at a glade with a homestead perched in the middle. The home appeared larger because it shared a wall with an adjacent barn. Titus couldn't make out details as his vision blurred. The blood loss and extreme pain had taken its toll.

Harold tapped the side of his horse with his heels, and the animal trotted out from the canopy of trees. The war veteran swiveled his head in all directions in case anyone raced out to attack, but no one came. The horse neighed in relief as it moseyed up to a water barrel and began slurping the liquid.

A man and a woman exited the house with wide, confused eyes.

"Good afternoon," Harold said, trying to project a calm and genteel manner. "To whom do I have the pleasure of speaking?"

Titus lifted his chin and found a middle-aged man wearing cotton stockings and a simple tan tunic. His scowl revealed his opinion of the intrusion.

"I'm Dicun." He pointed to himself and then flicked his wrist toward the woman. "This is my wife, Rosalind."

The woman wore a dress, similar to her husband's tunic, only longer.

"Dicun and Rosalind, I am Sir Harold of Chestershire, a knight proudly serving our king," he said with intentional pomp.

Dicun and Rosalind both bowed their heads. "My lord."

"This man is injured. I need you to swear before God Almighty that you will do everything in your power to care for him and protect him. Do you swear to do that?"

Dicun glanced at Titus. "Of course, my lord."

Titus's mind swirled as the impact of Harold's words registered. He was going to be left with these strangers.

Harold dismounted. Titus almost fell over without his support, but Harold steadied him with one hand and waved Dicun over with the other. They eased Titus off the horse and carried him toward the house. It wasn't easy carrying a man with an arrow in his right shoulder and thigh, but Harold went under his left shoulder and lifted Titus like he was a giant sack of wheat while Dicun lifted his left leg from behind leaving the right dragging in the dirt.

Titus whispered in Harold's ear. "You can't leave."

"There's no other choice. There may be others who need help. I must try to save them," Harold said.

Titus wanted to protest further, but he lacked the strength. They had no way of knowing whether Dicun and Rosalind were loyal to Kensington, Marmaduke, or anyone else.

Harold must have known this, too, because he craned his neck back toward Dicun. "You will be rewarded if you save him. Do not let Marmaduke's men get him." Harold pointed a finger at Dicun to emphasize the importance of his words and to suggest that failure would result in the opposite of a reward.

Dicun swallowed and wobbled as he carried Titus's leg.

Harold offered Titus an awkward smile, as if to show he'd taken care of any concerns.

Titus's vision faded in and out. It wouldn't be long before he slipped unconscious. This was going to happen. He was going to be abandoned and there was nothing he could do about it.

Harold and Dicun carried him inside and placed Titus on a bed with his right leg dangling off. As his body eased onto the mattress stuffed with straw and feathers, Titus felt a peace. The home was warm and the bed soft despite his clunky armor. Perhaps these were nice, loyal people, after all. He let down his guard and passed out, but the rest wasn't long or relaxing as the pain from his injuries caused him to slip in and out of consciousness.

When his eyes slid open, Dicun and Rosalind argued. Later, hands grabbed and pushed on him. Or maybe he was dreaming. Pieces of his armor clanged together. The arrow wounds ached and throbbed. *Was he moving?* The warmth he'd felt disappeared, and his body became cold. He thought to himself, *maybe this happens when you die. You get cold and then…*

His mind went blank.

CHAPTER 11

A door slammed shut and Titus's eyes popped open. A dark moist snout sniffed his face. He recoiled, causing pain to shoot through his injured arm and leg. Titus attempted to pick himself up, but his healthy arm failed him.

As he gathered his senses, he got a good look at the snout. It belonged to a tiny goat with speckled black and white fur. The animal chewed on a mouthful of hay while staring at Titus as if to say, "Who are you and why are you in my house?"

Titus assessed his surroundings. He was no longer on a comfortable bed. Instead, he lay on a pile of straw. Across the room, a beaten down horse with mangy gray hair laid on the ground of what Titus could only assume was the barn.

Feet shuffled on the other side of the wall and Dicun's gruff voice snapped, "How could this happen to us?"

"How long are you going to complain about it?" Rosalind asked.

"Watch your tongue, woman."

Rosalind didn't respond.

Dicun continued, "We need to know what happened in the

battle. That soldier must be very important to both sides. Did you see his armor? Do you know how much that is worth?"

Titus remained quiet and listened to the muffled argument from the barn. Dicun's shoes shuffled again across the wooden floor.

"If he dies, who knows what Kensington will do?" Dicun complained. "And what if Marmaduke's men come?" His nervous feet paced from one side of the home to the other. "If Marmaduke finds him, we'll be killed, and I'm not dying for that heap."

"Even if Marmaduke only believes we helped Kensington, we'll be killed, so we better make sure he's hidden well," Rosalind said in a stern, no nonsense tone.

"Or we get rid of him," Dicun said. "He's probably going to die, anyway. You saw how badly he was injured."

Footsteps bounded across the wood.

"What are you doing?" Dicun asked.

"You made an oath before God," Rosalind said.

"Don't take my mead."

"You have plenty to drink. The sooner we get him healed. The sooner he leaves."

"Don't talk back to me."

The door slammed shut. Seconds later, Rosalind opened the barn door carrying a mug, a large jar, and a blanket. She knelt beside Titus and poured a thick liquid from the jar into the cup. Titus lifted his head as she held the cup to his lips. He took a swig and grimaced at the foul taste.

"It's my husband's. For getting drunk. It tastes like piss and is probably made from it, too, but it will help the pain. And hopefully, it stops the rot from setting in." Rosalind began unstrapping the armor from the uninjured arm and leg. She'd never handled armor before, but that didn't stop her. Rosalind inspected each piece until she found the strap, untied it, and tossed the metal in the corner.

When she removed the leather sheath with Titus's dagger, he whispered. "I need that."

"Not right now, you don't."

Titus didn't have the strength to challenge her, so she continued turning the soldier into a patient until only two pieces of armor remained—the pauldron on his injured shoulder and the cuisses on the right thigh. Arrows had pierced both, wedging them against Titus's flesh. When the day started, the polished metal sparkled, but now it was dull with stained blood.

Rosalind searched the barn floor until she found a small rake with a thin wooden handle, which she offered.

Titus nodded. He'd been around enough battlefields and the aftermath to know what was coming. "Do you know what you're doing?" His voice cracked.

Rosalind raised an eyebrow. "Does it matter? You don't have a choice."

Titus placed the handle in his mouth and laid flat on his back.

"With any luck, you'll pass out when I pull the arrow out of your thigh." Rosalind didn't give Titus time to consider the implications of the statement and yanked.

Titus groaned and almost bit through the wood, but he did not pass out.

Rosalind wiped a bead of sweat off her forehead. "Guess we're not lucky."

Titus spit the stick out, and his chest heaved up and down from the pain.

"Stick back in. I need to clean the wound and wrap it."

Titus obeyed and clamped down, preparing for more anguish.

Rosalind removed the cuisses and tore the legging underneath, exposing the bloody mangled flesh. She lifted the jar and poured the mead on the wound.

Titus whimpered and moaned.

Rosalind grabbed the blanket she'd brought and cut a strip off the end. She tied it tight around the wound to prevent it from bleeding, but not so tight as to cut off the blood flow. She drizzled more of the brown liquid over the wrap, which elicited more groans.

"Halfway there."

Titus shook his head for her to stop, but Rosalind knew better than to drag it out. She gripped the arrow from Titus's shoulder and yanked. This time, Titus found luck and passed out.

TITUS'S EYES LULLED OPEN. He stared at the thatched roof over his head, confused. It didn't look like his home. He tried to move, but the shooting pain from his arm and leg reminded him of the battle and the aftermath. His dry throat begged for water. When he noticed a cup near his uninjured arm, it was as if an angel had heard his cry. He brought it to his lips, sipping at first, but the liquid tasted so good, he gulped the rest. On the other side of the stable, the old horse munched on some grass in a bin. The tiny goat paced around the area, stopped, and lifted its head toward Titus.

"What are you looking at?" Titus asked.

The goat "baa'd" and went to the other side of the barn.

Aside from the horse and goat, the barn housed a coup with two chickens. Straw blanketed the floor, and he lay in the thickest section.

As Titus gathered his senses, his hands grazed a tawny blanket that covered him, but otherwise, he was naked, except for a portion of his leggings that still concealed his nether regions.

Titus craned his neck against his chest to inspect his injured shoulder. The wool wrap didn't have blood bleeding through it —a good sign, but Titus knew that if pestilence set in, he'd soon be dead.

In the prior war, he'd watched men emerge from battle with minor wounds, only to die a couple of weeks later. An infected cut turned a dark green or a deep purple and eventually it became black. When Titus had to carry his wife's body for burial, giant black sores covered her arms. He poked his shoulder to test it. The injury still ached, but it was too soon to know if disease had set in.

Feet trundled inside the house, and then the door creaked open. Titus peered through the gaps in the rotting wooden planks of the wall. Dicun marched out with a bow slung over his shoulder. A moment later, he flung the barn door open. Upon finding Titus awake, he huffed, shuffled inside, and snatched the reins of the horse.

"Come on, Bucktooth." Dicun yanked the reins and led the horse out. The animal neighed in protest, and its front teeth jutted out, no doubt the inspiration for its name.

Once outside, Dicun mounted the old nag and rode down a trail. As soon as he was out of sight, Rosalind opened the barn door.

"Look who's up."

"How long has it been?" Titus asked.

"Only a couple of days. You drifted in and out. Are you hungry?"

Titus considered the question and then realized he was starving. He nodded.

Rosalind disappeared and returned with a petite bread loaf and some salted venison. She handed it to Titus, who snatched it and gnawed on the tough meat like it was the last piece of food on earth. He closed his eyes and savored the saltiness. "Thank you."

Rosalind grabbed Titus's empty cup, went back to the house, and then came back with it filled.

"Thank you," he said again before gulping its contents. Water never tasted so good. As he chewed another bite of meat, he nodded his head toward the trail where Dicun had left. "Your husband is a kind one."

Rosalind raised an eyebrow. "You don't exactly seem like you're made of peaches and strawberries."

Titus bowed his head in remorse. "Apologies for my comment."

Rosalind stared down the trail. "And he's just scared."

"And you're not?"

"We deal with things differently." Rosalind changed the subject, uninterested in sharing personal details with a stranger. "So, what happened?"

Titus tore the bread in half while remembering the unfortunate events. "There was a battle."

Rosalind lowered her eyes with a scolding gaze at the obvious statement.

Titus nodded. "The battle didn't go as planned. Kensington's army lost."

"How bad?"

"I don't know."

"Is Marmaduke the new king?" she asked.

"I don't think so."

"Can Kensington come back?"

Titus shoved half the loaf in his mouth and chewed while considering the question. "If he's still alive, there's a chance." The blanket fell, revealing Titus's bare chest. When he reached down to pull it up, a panic set in. He patted his sides, but all he felt were the tatters from his leggings. He flung the surrounding straw. "Where's my dagger?"

"It's inside the house."

Titus stopped searching and turned to Rosalind. "I need it."

"Dicun wasn't comfortable with you having a weapon."

"I *need* it," he said again.

A stand-off resulted with both man and woman glaring at the other.

Rosalind took a deep breath and huffed, but she returned to the house, and when she came back, she held the dagger with both hands. She bit her lower lip and offered it to Titus.

"Thank you." Titus grabbed the handle and stared at his prized possession before placing it in the straw beside him. When he looked up, the door shut and Rosalind was gone.

THE REST of the afternoon dragged. Titus tried to move, but neither his shoulder nor thigh allowed more than a wriggle to ease the worst discomfort. The highlight of the day came when Rosalind brought a cup of ale and a strip of dried venison.

Besides that, Titus stared at the goat, chickens, or dagger. None held his interest. The goat ambled about the barn, munching on straw. It seemed to know instinctively Titus was injured and harmless. The dagger also knew, and every time Titus fixed his eyes on the blade, it taunted him. *You can't hurt anyone, let alone Marmaduke, the future king and the man who killed your only son*. In his current condition, Titus not only couldn't fight, he couldn't do much of anything.

Late in the afternoon, Dicun emerged from the forest atop Bucktooth. Titus studied the trees and trail behind Dicun to make sure he wasn't followed. The cantankerous oaf struck

Titus as the type to rat him out to Marmaduke's men, but thankfully, no one else came.

Dicun guided the horse back to the barn with a dead rabbit slung off the side. Rosalind met him in front, but neither spoke. She took the slain animal and brought it inside. He slid off the horse, grabbed the reins, and walked the beast to the barn. Dicun swung the door open and smacked the back of the old horse. "Get in there."

The toothy animal retreated to its bed of hay, eager to avoid the company of its irascible owner. Dicun shut the door and left, ignoring Titus.

Titus leaned his ear against the wall connected to the house. At first, no one spoke, but muffled conversation soon started. Dicun's deep voice growled and sputtered while Rosalind's melted into the background. Titus couldn't make out any words until Dicun shouted. "You did what?" A loud smack followed, and then the front door slammed shut.

Titus tried to shift to a less conspicuous position, but he was too slow. The barn door flew open.

Dicun stepped inside with wide eyes and flaring nostrils. "You having a good listen there, friend? Give me the dagger." He held out his hand, but didn't step closer.

Even in his weakened state, Titus could smell Dicun's fear, despite the display of bravado.

"I said, give me the dagger."

Titus weighed his options. He didn't want to encourage Dicun to seek Marmaduke, but he also would not follow orders from an insufferable fool.

"You like receiving food every day?" Dicun asked.

"The dagger…means something to me. I must have it." With nothing more than a stern gaze, Titus dared Dicun to take it.

Dicun puffed out his chest and lifted his nose while looking down at Titus. "I'm not afraid of you."

"Never said you were." But Titus knew he was. "What happened in there? What was that noise?" Titus motioned with his head toward the house.

Dicun sneered and slammed the door shut. He huffed back inside the home and slammed that door, too.

For the rest of the evening, Titus listened to Dicun berate Rosalind. A heavy guilt weighed on him and convinced him of one thing. He had to get better fast and leave, for everyone's sake.

CHAPTER 12

Rosalind opened the barn door carrying a fresh cup of ale and two pieces of bread. She placed them beside Titus, who stirred from his slumber and shielded his eyes from the light streaming through the doorway.

"Thank you," he said.

Rosalind didn't respond, and when she turned, it revealed a deep bruise on the left side of her face. Anger filled Titus's stomach, and he sat up. He wanted to say something, apologize maybe, and he definitely wanted to pummel Dicun, but Rosalind slipped out before he uttered a word.

Once again, Titus found himself alone, except for the animals to keep him company. Unfortunately, they weren't much for conversation, despite the goat's incessant "baas".

As he evaluated his injuries, he couldn't help but think about what Harold said before they departed for the final battle. "*You don't know what's going to happen, Titus.*" His friend was right. Titus never would've predicted his current situation—injured and alone in a strange farmhouse after losing in battle.

The barn itself reminded him of his wife, Ariella. She spent her last days in their barn. Titus had wanted to sit with her, but she made him promise that he wouldn't go inside. She said the risk of spreading the sickness to Aidan and him was too great, so Titus did the only other thing he could think of. He pulled up a small wooden stool and sat outside the barn door. On the first day, he kept her spirit up by talking, but on the second day, her wheezing and coughing had intensified. Late on the third day, Titus sat with his back against the barn's wall and Ariella's raspy voice called out. "Titus."

"Yes, my love."

"Promise me—," she hacked and sputtered as she tried to speak. "Promise me you'll take care of Aidan." Those were her last words.

A tear rolled down Titus's cheek as he relived the painful memory. He couldn't even honor his wife's dying wish. Before he could wallow in his misery any longer, armed soldiers appeared at the fringe of the tree line. Titus jolted upright. He didn't need to wonder who they were. Their black leather armor gave them away.

Panicked feet stomped on the other side of the wall, followed by Dicun's scared voice. "Tell them… I've gone hunting." Footsteps scampered off into the trees behind the house.

Titus's eyes darted around the barn. There couldn't be any hint of his presence, but there were signs everywhere—his armor in the corner, the blanket, the dagger in the hay, and the empty cup.

If the soldiers found him, they'd kill him for sure and there's no telling what they'd do to Rosalind. Half-naked, he pulled himself to his feet and hobbled to the armor. With his healthy arm, he shoved straw over it and assessed the result. Not good enough.

Marmaduke's men swayed atop their horses as they trotted down the path. Titus was running out of time. He tossed the blanket over the armor, hoping no one would look underneath.

With his good arm, he scooped up his dagger, cup, and bread and hobbled to the back corner of the barn, where the old horse lay on its side. He nestled on the backside of Bucktooth, which snorted from the disturbance.

"It's okay," Titus whispered. He brushed straw over his feet and pulled himself tight against the animal, praying it didn't move.

The door of the home creaked open. "Hello? What can I do for you?" Rosalind asked.

Titus lifted his head so he could see above the hulking mound of the horse's side. Through the cracks in the planks, Titus counted three men, including Enok, the gargantuan henchman from Marmaduke's army.

"Where is your husband?" Enok asked.

"He's not here right now. He's left for the day to go hunting."

"Have any soldiers sought quarter with you?" Enok asked.

"No. Why would they?"

"God found favor with Marmaduke and delivered Kensington's wretched army into his hands. They were routed, and many cowards fled."

"That is wonderful news," Rosalind said.

"Marmaduke is now the king. You shall serve him and pay homage."

"Of course."

Titus listened to the exchange and watched what he could through the cracks. One soldier hopped off his horse and entered the house. The other guided his animal to the rear of the home.

"Is your husband fit for military service?"

"Why is he needed if Kensington's army has been routed?"

Enok raised his voice. "Are you talking back to me?"

"No, my lord. It was just a question?"

The goat sniffed the bed of straw where Titus had been, perhaps finding a few scraps from his meals. It then drifted over to the corner where the blanket covered the armor.

Titus waved his hand to get the goat's attention, but it found the fabric far too fascinating. It nuzzled against the soft material, causing some of the armor underneath to shift and clank together.

Enok dismounted. "Is someone in the barn?"

"Just animals," Rosalind said, her voice rising with panic.

Titus ducked his head down as the door flung open.

The goat "baa'd" and stomped at the ground.

"See, just a goat," Rosalind said.

Titus laid deathly still, which was ironic because that would be his fate if the horse moved.

Enok surveyed the simple barn. "Your husband left his steed to go hunting?"

"Bucktooth?" Rosalind swatted the air in the horse's direction. "Look at that old bag."

Silence followed. Titus kept his head lowered, and he could only hope Enok was satisfied with the answers and leave, but he wasn't.

"What are you looking at?" Rosalind asked.

"You," Enok said.

A chill went down Titus's spine.

"What happened to your face?"

"I tripped and hit the side of the table."

Enok grunted without revealing his opinion of the answer.

"Your husband leaves you here all alone, does he?"

"Please. Don't touch me."

"You're very close to testing my nerves, my lady."

"My husband will be back soon, I'm sure of it."

Titus gripped his dagger and prepared to attack. He was no match for Enok in his current condition. His only chance was surprise, but even if he somehow felled Enok, he still had to contend with the two soldiers outside. But he had to act. Titus took a deep breath and counted down in his head. *Three... two...*

"Enok. Let's go. We've got other homes to check," one soldier shouted.

Enok grunted with frustration and then left. Titus let out an exhale of relief.

DICUN WAITED until evening before returning. The coward slipped into the back of the house the way he'd fled.

Titus slid against the wall separating the barn from the home and eavesdropped. It wasn't as hard to hear the conversation this time as Rosalind shouted at her husband for deserting her.

Dicun took the news of his wife's near assault rather well. He did not take the news of Kensington's loss the same.

His heels clopped against the wooden floor, pacing back and forth. "We need to know if Marmaduke really is the king."

"Why must we know this?"

"We can't keep feeding and protecting this soldier if it's going to get us killed."

"Are you gonna cast him out into the forest to die?"

Silence followed until Dicun spoke again. "I will leave in the morning to find out for certain what has happened."

"You're leaving. Again! After what happened?"

A loud smack, and then nothing. Titus moved his ear away from the wall.

CHAPTER 13

The red sun peeked over the eastern horizon, bringing the world to life, both peaceful creatures and unsavory ones like Dicun. The hungover man awoke and entered the barn with bags under his eyes. He ignored Titus and stumbled to Bucktooth, which lay on its side, mouth open, and teeth hanging out. The creature snorted upon seeing his master and forced itself on all fours. True to his word, Dicun led Bucktooth outside, mounted it, and rode away, leaving his wife alone for the second straight day.

Titus leaned up and his heartbeat pulsed through his shoulder, each beat causing it to throb. *Was that normal?* The idea of getting sick ate at him, as he'd witnessed such a horror first-hand.

When his stomach rumbled for nourishment, it was a welcome distraction. He assumed Rosalind would bring food any minute, but she didn't. Time passed and Titus continued to wait. *Was she okay?*

Titus wrapped himself in the blanket, pulled himself to his feet, and took two small steps before his knees buckled. He steadied himself and hobbled out of the barn. It was the first time he'd left the stable since being dumped into the bed of straw, and the morning sunlight forced him to squint as his eyes adjusted. Titus tapped on the door with two fingers.

No response.

He tugged on the handle and the door cracked opened. The first time he entered the home, he was near death and didn't get a good look at it, but he did now. Everything was clean and organized. The quaint interior had sanded wooden floors, a rare luxury, and a cedar cupboard.

With her back to Titus, Rosalind rested on a chair beside the hearth, where the tiniest of flames consumed the remnant of a log. She didn't react to his uninvited visit.

"Would you mind if I got a cup of ale?" Titus asked.

"In the barrel," Rosalind said, without turning around.

Titus hobbled to a table with a small cask on top. Three other barrels were stacked beside the table. "When will your husband return?"

"I don't know." She craned her neck ever so slightly and glanced back.

Titus looked to the left of the table, then to the right, but he couldn't find a cup. "Will he turn me in if Marmaduke is king?" He opened the cupboard, revealing a small collection of coats, leggings, and tunics.

"I don't know," Rosalind said again. She shook her head as he fumbled through her home. When she couldn't take it anymore, she jumped to her feet and reached down under the table where four cups hung on hooks. She handed one to Titus.

"Thank you," he said, embarrassed.

Rosalind looked away, but it was too late. Titus caught sight of the deep purple and black bruise on her cheek.

"Does that happen often?" Titus motioned to the injury.

Rosalind's piercing glance didn't answer the question, but it sent a clear message for Titus to drop the subject.

"If Marmaduke's man returns, I will fight him."

"A lot of good that will do." Rosalind shook her head as she eyed his pathetic condition and then walked back to her chair by the hearth.

"I would've fought the soldiers if they…"

"Well, then we'd both be dead." Rosalind pointed to a second table beside her with a basket on top. "There's some bread if you're hungry."

Titus poured a glass of ale and then shuffled to the table. He paused before taking a small loaf. He walked awkwardly with the cup and bread in one hand while trying to keep the blanket tucked over his shoulders, but he managed the feat and retreated to the barn.

Titus nibbled at the food while thinking about his predicament. He had to get healthy so he could leave.

As he sipped the ale, Rosalind opened the door and marched in, carrying a barrel with a cloth and tunic on top of it. With her arms straining, she heaved the drum onto the small stool with the spigot facing Titus. "No need to come inside anymore."

Titus nodded. She wanted him to leave as quickly as possible, too.

Rosalind grabbed the cloth off the top. "Let's see how the injuries are looking." She didn't wait for Titus to accept her offer and pulled down the blanket covering his right shoulder. Rosalind unwrapped the bandage, revealing mangled and scabbed flesh with dark green edges.

Rosalind touched the surrounding skin. She sighed. "It's warm."

"Has a sickness set in?"

"Yes." Rosalind opened the spigot and dripped ale on the strip of cloth and then re-wrapped the injury.

"Will that take care of it?"

"No."

The answer hit Titus like a punch, spinning his world.

Marmaduke had already killed him. "So, that's it then? I'm a dead man?"

Rosalind remained silent for a long moment. "I may be able to treat it if I get some sage and honey from the medicine woman."

"Where is she?" Titus asked.

"She's a half day's hike away near Vassar Springs."

"Vassar Spring? That's in the Southern Territory. I can't ask you to do that."

"You certainly can't do it," Rosalind snapped. Before leaving, she tossed the tunic by Titus's side.

"Is this Dicun's?" Titus asked.

Rosalind didn't respond.

"Will this cause you trouble?"

"Not as much trouble as you dying or running around here half-naked."

Rosalind left the barn, and within minutes, she hiked down the trail with a small bag slung over her shoulder.

EVENING ROLLED into night and the barn became almost pitch black. The only light came from the faintest rays of moonlight seeping through the cracks in the walls.

The darkness might've made for a peaceful sleep, but his throbbing shoulder foiled any opportunity for rest. The flesh burned from the sickness that worsened by the minute. He continued sipping the ale to mask the pain, but a heavy drink could only do so much. If he avoided focusing on his discomfort, he was left with his thoughts, which weren't any better. The idea of Rosalind hiking alone, especially for his sake, troubled him. She'd already been gone for several hours. What if something happened to her? And what if Dicun returned with Marmaduke's men?

Titus took a gulp of ale, and an emptiness settled into the pit of his stomach that wasn't caused by lack of food or drink. A tear slid down his cheek as he stared at his own mortality in the blackness. The void. All the battles he'd fought had amounted to nothing. His wife and son had died for no reason. He'd been abandoned, all alone in the dark, save for a goat and some chickens, in a filthy barn. He would die, just as his wife had, from a disease that tortured his body before taking any shred of dignity he had left.

One random thought provided a speck of light in the darkness —a memory of Ariella teaching him to read. During one of their first winters together, a heavy storm pounded their little home, but they remained warm and dry. Learning to read as an adult proved challenging for Titus, and he would have been embarrassed if he had been with anyone but her. Instead, he experienced a peace unlike any he'd ever felt. Ariella's Bible lay on his lap, but his brain struggled to connect the letters to words and words to sentences. She helped him sound out the words as his finger guided his eyes.

"When you pass through the waters," she said, as Titus muttered in unison under his breath. She stopped and let him continue alone. "I will be with you; and when you pass through the rivers, they will not sweep over you." His choppy reading was unsure, and each word struggled to come out of his mouth. "When you walk through the fire, you will not be burned; the flames will not set you ablaze."

As Titus enjoyed the comfort of that memory, he considered the words from the verse. Anger and resentment replaced his fleeting moment of calm. If God was with him, where was He now? Like everything in his life, did all those words mean nothing, too?

Something stirred outside. Titus sat up and listened. Footsteps lumbered along the dirt path. Titus clenched his dagger against his chest.

The door to the house opened and feet shuffled against the floor. Maybe Dicun or Rosalind had returned. Titus leaned his ear against the wall. The wooden boards creaked from the soft steps before falling silent. Titus considered going into the house, but decided against it. If it was Dicun, he wouldn't want him there, and if it was Rosalind, he might scare her. If it was anyone else, he wasn't strong enough to fight. The individual stirred again and left the home. An orange glow approached the barn. The door opened. Rosalind carried a lantern along with a jar and cup.

Titus was about to open his mouth, but no words came out. Instead, he studied Rosalind. Her eyes had giant bags under them, but she refused to give in to the fatigue, placing everything on the floor. Rosalind didn't speak as she pulled down the blanket and unwrapped Titus's injured shoulder. Even in the limited light, it was clear the wound had gotten worse as the dark green invaded more of the flesh. Rosalind covered her finger in the honey and then dipped it into the cup so that crushed sage stuck to it. She smeared the concoction over the gash.

His shoulder should've hurt when she touched it, but it didn't. Maybe it was the medicine or maybe it was her gentle fingers gliding over the wound, but there was no pain.

Rosalind applied two swabs and then moved onto his thigh. He had to roll away from her awkwardly, but her light touch put him at ease. She placed a clean corner of the blanket under the injury as he rolled back.

"We will not wrap it tonight," she said in a whisper. "The medicine woman said to avoid getting anything on it as much as possible." Rosalind wiped her hands on her tunic, gathered the things, and left without saying another word.

Titus wanted to speak. A "thank you" would've been more than appropriate, but he laid there in stunned silence. The woman had risked her life, and she'd hiked the entire day to the point of exhaustion, but she didn't wait until morning to treat him.

It was impossible for medicine to work that fast, but somehow Titus knew she'd saved him.

CHAPTER 14

Larks trilled, stirring Titus from his sleep. His eyes opened with hope, and he inspected his wounds. The dried honey covered the gashes, but the surrounding skin had streaks of pale, healthy tissue invading the dark green infection. The medicine was working!

Titus still had a long road ahead, but he at least had a chance now. He tapped his fingers against his thigh while waiting for Rosalind. Not only was he hungry, but he also wanted to show her the wound and thank her. Titus considered going into the house, but she'd made her opinion on that very clear. He coughed intentionally loud, but she didn't come. Taking it further, he reached over and knocked his armor so it clattered together.

Feet shuffled inside. Titus smiled.

Moments later, Rosalind entered with a loaf of bread, the jar, and sage. "Assume you're feeling better if you're making all that noise?"

"Yes, and I wanted to—"

"Good. When can you leave?" she asked.

Her bluntness caught Titus off guard, but then he remembered Dicun, and Rosalind's bruised face still showed the impact of his imposition.

Titus pulled himself to his feet and his healthy leg quivered. A night of drinking was not helpful for balance. When he steadied himself, he shifted his weight to his injured leg. A shooting pain jolted his senses, causing his legs to buckle. He leaned against the wall for support.

Rosalind exhaled with frustration. "You're not walking out of here for a while."

"I'm sorry for getting shot."

"Twice," Rosalind added. "Sit back down."

Titus followed the order and Rosalind sat beside him. She wiped away the dried honey and then dipped her finger in the jar and cup for a fresh application.

Titus wanted to say something, but his mouth kept opening and closing with nothing coming out.

"What is it?" she asked.

Titus blurted, "Do you want my help?"

Rosalind furrowed her brow. "With what?"

"With your husband?"

Rosalind chuckled under her breath. "What are you going to do?" She waved toward his injuries before dabbing her finger across his shoulder with the honey.

"I've seen your husband. I can help," Titus said, mildly insulted by Rosalind's comment. "Fighting may be the only thing I'm good at."

"Maybe you're not as good as you think." Rosalind offered a dismissive glance at the heap in front of her and then made direct eye contact. "You best mind your business," she said in a calm but stern voice.

Titus nodded, accepting her rejection.

When Rosalind finished applying the honey to Titus's thigh, she collected the jar and cup, stood, and left. As soon as she was gone, Titus's depression from the night before returned. He didn't like being alone. He also didn't like being helpless and useless.

After feeling sorry for himself, Titus pulled himself to his feet. This time, he eased some of his weight onto the right leg and then shuffled forward a few inches. It hurt, but it was manageable. He continued the process and limped out of the barn.

Once outside, a sloshing sound from the other side of the house lured Titus. He hobbled over and found Rosalind rinsing clothes in a barrel. She paused as he stumbled over. "What are you doing?" she asked.

Titus struggled for a response. "I wanted to… strengthen my leg and get some water."

"In the house. Second rundlet."

Titus turned to leave, but he didn't want a drink, so he faced Rosalind again.

"Now what?" she asked.

"Why did you help me?" He genuinely didn't know. She clearly didn't like him. He was a threat to her life, and he'd already caused plenty of trouble with her husband.

"You needed it," she said. "And there was no one else that was going to do it." Her simple answer made sense, and yet, it didn't. He was a total stranger. Most people would've reacted like Dicun. If Rosalind had not made the trek for medicine, he might be dead or very near.

"Can I help?" Titus asked. He glanced at Rosalind, then at the clothes.

Rosalind stopped. "With this?" She motioned to the wet tunic, perplexed.

Titus nodded. He'd never been above any activity and he

wasn't pretending that laundry somehow equaled what Rosalind had done. He got on his knees and gritted his teeth from the pain, but did his best to mask it.

"You sure you're up for this?"

"It's good to work the shoulder out. So I can leave sooner, of course."

Rosalind handed him a bar of soap made from ash and animal fat. Titus held it in his left hand and placed his right on the edge of the tub for balance. He got to work and scrubbed the soap against the sopping cloth by wedging it against the side of the wooden cask.

Rosalind watched him. "Hmm. Better than I expected."

"I've done my share of washing clothes."

"Really?"

"After my wife died, I had a choice. Learn or my son and I would've become the smelliest farmers in the Northern Territory."

"You had a wife?" she asked with surprise but didn't intend for it to sound so insulting.

Titus took no offense. "Yes, but she died from the plague."

"I'm sorry." A moment of awkward silence followed. "How old is your son?"

"He was thirteen."

"The plague also?"

Titus shook his head and averted his gaze.

"I'm sorry," Rosalind said again, but in the softest, kindest voice. Until now, she'd spoken in either a gruff or cold tone. She dropped her chin to her chest and worked, perhaps afraid to ask another question that only had a painful answer. After a few minutes, she handed Titus a blanket to wash while she took the tunic he'd been working to wring out.

Titus soaked the large wool fabric and then scrubbed with the soap. He was happy to work, but mostly, he didn't want to be alone in the barn. "Do you think Dicun will come back with Marmaduke's men?"

Rosalind shrugged. "Dicun is...unpredictable."

"Yes. I've noticed." Titus paused his scrubbing and looked up at Rosalind. "May I ask how you came to be with him?"

"I come from a poor family. We didn't have much for a dowry."

Titus didn't need to press for details. Before he'd left to fight with Charles, he'd seen how that sort of marriage worked. A father of the potential bride would talk to the groom's father and negotiate for the smallest dowry possible. It wasn't abnormal for a young wife-to-be or groom to have little say in the matter of their spouse. Before Titus imagined the reasons Dicun might not be happy with Rosalind, she offered, "He wasn't always like this. He was a decent man at first. He used to read the Bible."

"Really? I wouldn't have pegged him for that."

"He's quite smart. He worked hard." Rosalind considered her own statement. "He still does, actually. He's a good provider. It's the drink. That's what changed him." She squeezed the tunic tighter and wrung out the last drops of water.

"He shouldn't hit you."

"We all have our issues." Rosalind carried the tunic over to a large bush and spread it over the branches so it could dry.

"Not like that."

"I could leave him, I suppose, but he didn't leave me, even when I couldn't bear him any children."

Titus continued to work on the blanket. His thoughts no longer focused on his wife, son, Marmaduke, or the war. They centered on Rosalind's precarious position. If she left Dicun, she'd be alone. No other man would take her if she couldn't have children. Titus wasn't going to stay, nor could he. Rosalind was trapped. He stared at her as she finished spreading the tunic out. When she turned around, he dropped his head and scrubbed.

Her footsteps shuffled along the dirt until she stood beside him. He glanced up and found her staring toward the trail.

"Dicun's back," she said.

CHAPTER 15

Bucktooth's hoofs clip clopped along the dirt path as it carried Dicun closer. Titus dropped the blanket he'd been cleaning and stood. Had Dicun sold him out? If he had, an enemy lurked nearby. The trees swayed in the wind, and Dicun continued down the trail.

Rosalind took one step toward her husband as if she was going to greet him, but then she stopped, and waited.

Dicun stared at Rosalind and Titus with a furrowed brow. Seeing them together and cleaning clothes, no less, must have surprised him. He dismounted and led the horse to the barn. A smack on the animal's rump sent Bucktooth trotting to its soft bed of hay. Dicun didn't say a word and disappeared inside the home.

Rosalind followed. "Dicun?"

Titus hobbled behind. When he opened the door, Dicun already had a cup of ale in his hand, ready to drown out reality. He collapsed in the oak chair by the hearth. Rosalind stood behind her husband, hands on her hips.

"Don't just sit there. Tell me what you found out," Rosalind said.

Dicun had no interest in his wife's pestering. He swatted the air as if her comments were flies. Dicun stopped when Titus entered and pulled his chair around. "What do you want?"

Despite his hobbled state, Titus's stern gaze demanded information, and Dicun had no desire to challenge him.

"Marmaduke isn't king," Dicun said, but then added, "yet." He took a long gulp of ale and wiped the dribble with his sleeve.

"Where is Kensington's army?" Titus asked.

"Not sure if you could call it that anymore, but what's left of it is under siege at Fennelworth Castle."

Titus shook his head. "Marmaduke doesn't have the manpower for a winter siege."

"He now has the support of Lord Chaucer and Lord Gilroy."

"Both of them?" Titus asked, incredulous.

"Marmaduke's forces killed Titus and that convinced them both of the side that would emerge victorious."

Titus didn't flinch when his name was uttered.

"Who is Titus?" Rosalind asked.

"He's the legend from the war against the three wicked barons. He'd never lost. Until now." Dicun stared at Titus, oblivious that the "legend" stood in front of him. In Titus's current state, he didn't match whatever Dicun had built up in his mind. Even if Titus was healthy, he wouldn't have fit Dicun's perception of the mighty warrior. "Did you know Titus was fighting with Kensington?" Dicun asked.

Titus considered his answer and offered a one-word response. "Yes."

"Was he killed?"

Titus didn't condone lying. He felt nobles did it far too often when the truth became inconvenient, but he couldn't reveal his identity to someone like Dicun. "Many people died in the fight." Titus rationalized that an omission of a direct answer didn't qualify as a lie, but even that pulled at his conscience.

Dicun took another healthy sip of ale and poured himself a second cup. "There will be a final battle or a surrender in spring. Maybe earlier if they run out of food."

TITUS LAY IN THE BARN, but he couldn't sleep. He twirled the dagger in his hand with a nervous energy. He had to return to Fennelworth before Kensington surrendered. If Lord Chaucer and Lord Gilroy received word that he was not dead, perhaps they might withdraw their support. He didn't know how he'd reunite with Kensington, as he could barely walk, but he had to do something.

When morning arrived, Rosalind delivered water and bread. She also brought more honey and sage for Titus's wounds. She leaned down and inspected his shoulder. "It looks much better."

"I need to leave. Today," Titus blurted. He wanted to tell her who he was and why he needed to go, but the words remained choked away.

Rosalind snorted and let out a slight chuckle, but the resolve in Titus's eyes silenced her.

Titus pulled himself up. "I need the horse." He hobbled over to the animal laying in the hay and patted its rear to bring it to its feet. He guided the steed toward the door, but stopped when he stood next to Rosalind. There was a mix of gratitude, guilt, sorrow, and fear. He wanted to say so many things to her, but all he could muster was, "I will return the animal. I promise." He led Bucktooth out of the barn.

Rosalind hurried into the house, and a moment later, Dicun rushed out. "Where do you think you're going with *my* horse?"

"Thank you for your hospitality, Dicun. It will be rewarded, and I *will* return your horse."

"You can't leave with him."

"I must. It's safer for you this way."

Dicun couldn't argue with the logic, but he still would not let Titus leave with his property. He stepped in front of the animal, leaving the two men facing one another.

Rosalind rushed out with a cloth she'd tied into a sack. "Some food and medicine for your travels."

Dicun glared at his wife like she'd betrayed him.

Titus accepted the gift with reservation and placed it above the horn on the saddle. "Thank you. May I have a word with your husband alone?"

Rosalind nodded and left.

Titus turned to Dicun. "I swear before God that your property will be returned by spring. Along with it, you'll receive a financial reward."

Dicun's eyes widened with intrigue. "How much?"

"How much do you want?"

"Five pieces of silver. Ten if you don't bring back the horse."

Titus paused as he considered the significant sum. "Alright. Then we shake on it."

Titus offered his hand. Dicun stared at it, but hesitated.

"We must seal the oath." Titus kept his palm out.

Dicun extended his hand and shook. Titus's grip tightened like a python, causing Dicun to panic. "What are you doing?"

Titus stared at him like a starving lion. He waited until he had direct eye contact with Dicun. "Do you want me to hit you?"

Dicun shook his head and tried to pull away, but he couldn't.

"It would hurt, wouldn't it?"

Dicun nodded.

Titus squeezed harder. "I could kill you, couldn't I?

Dicun swallowed.

"Would you like to live like that—wondering if or when I'm going to hurt you?"

Dicun averted his gaze.

"We made an oath before God. You'll get your money, but I also swear that if you hurt her again, you will swallow every one of those pieces of silver." Titus shoved Dicun backward, and he tumbled to the ground.

Dicun didn't get up. Instead, he rubbed his hand and kept his head lowered. His cowardice had been called out.

Titus placed his left foot in the stirrup and mounted the horse. He winced as he eased his right thigh into the saddle. Dicun remained on the dirt in shame as Titus rode down the trail.

CHAPTER 16

The frigid air chilled Titus to the bone as he rode Bucktooth along the trail in a heavy mist. Each step jostled his injuries and brought a throbbing ache. After an hour of riding, the pain became too much, and he stopped. He dismounted and stretched his left arm. Then he tried his right. As soon as his shoulder extended above ninety degrees, a searing pain shot down the length of his arm. Titus gritted his teeth and pushed his palm higher until he almost passed out. He needed his mobility back. He then lifted his knee to stretch his injured thigh and a wrenching sting left him nauseous. If anyone found him, let alone Marmaduke's men, there was little he could do to defend himself.

Other doubts plagued him, too. If the castle was surrounded, as Dicun described, how could he get a message inside? It also wouldn't be of much benefit to the men if they only knew he was alive. He needed to break the siege.

The goal of a siege was to starve the castle's defenders into submission. Since winter had just begun, Kensington's men had enough food for now, but the cold season was long in the

Northern Territory. At some point, they would run out, which meant a surrender or a battle.

Titus could only pray he'd come up with an idea to help before he reached the castle, a mere fifteen miles away. Of course, at his snail's pace, it would take two days, so there'd be plenty of time for reflection. As he was about to remount the old horse, he froze.

The ground trembled. Someone was coming!

Titus hurried off the trail while tugging the reins and leading Bucktooth into the foliage. He guided the animal behind a thick tree and knelt down. Hoofs clapped against the earth and echoed through the trees. Within seconds, two knights emerged on horseback, pulling a carriage of supplies. Each wore shiny chain mail. *Was it Kensington's men?* Titus considered revealing himself until he noticed the telltale black leather armor under the metal. They were Marmaduke's forces.

His shoulders slumped as he waited for them to pass. The fact they now had chain mail verified they'd gotten additional support. Titus returned to the trail, mounted the horse, and continued his journey.

After a couple more hours, the sun dipped in the sky, which cast the forest in shadows. It would be dark soon, and Titus needed to find a safe place to sleep before that happened. He slid off Bucktooth and led the animal into the trees. A day of riding left his entire backside sore. Leaves and twigs cracked under his hobbled steps until he discovered a small clearing amid a cluster of rocks. A low branch from a giant evergreen extended over the site and offered a partial canopy from the elements. Such a simple campsite never looked so appealing.

Titus tied the reins to the tree and then carried the satchel of sustenance Rosalind prepared to a large rock. He wasn't the only one who needed food, as Bucktooth sniffed the area for any grass and shrubs. The wind rustled the leaves as Titus eased his leg down and leaned his back against the granite slab. He opened the satchel, removed the honey and sage, and applied it to his injuries. The long day of travel left him exhausted and in pain, but his mobility had improved. As he settled in for the night, he enjoyed a strip of salted venison and a half loaf of bread. He savored each bite, knowing he was unlikely to find more food soon. Rosalind had packed two more strips and one other loaf, which he saved for the rest of the trek.

When the sun set, darkness blanketed the forest except for a sliver of moonlight that pierced through the trees. Like his nights in the barn, Titus was alone, except for Bucktooth. The old horse settled down a few feet away. Titus crawled over and laid his head against the animal's side. The steady expansion and contraction of Bucktooth's midsection as it breathed lulled Titus to sleep and dreams of happier times with his wife and son. If given the choice, he would've stayed in those memories forever, but life was not that kind. Something tugged at his subconscious and told him to wake up. His eyes slid open and a jolt of alarm surged through his veins. A human figure crept out of the shadows toward his tiny camp. Every fiber of Titus's being wanted to fight or flee, but he forced himself to lie still and pretend to sleep.

The interloper stepped closer.

Thieves and bandits roamed the forest, waiting for travelers to prey upon. Titus wondered how long he'd been followed and if there were others. His dagger remained tucked inside his hem if he needed to defend himself, but he hoped the intruder would realize he had little of value and leave without a confrontation.

The prowler slithered closer and his slight frame gave Titus comfort. He'd have a chance if it came to a fight. Nothing else moved in the trees, which further bolstered his confidence. The creeper crouched low and inched into the clearing by the rock.

He revealed his intentions when he reached for the satchel of food and honey, only inches away from Titus.

The meat and bread were all Titus had to survive. He wasn't in the best condition to fight, but he couldn't afford to lose his remaining nourishment or medicine. In a flash, Titus struck like a viper, despite the pain from his injuries. He grabbed the thief's hand and pounced on top of him.

The figure yowled in surprise and tried to wrestle free. "Don't hurt me."

Titus realized it was a boy, and no match for him, but with only one healthy arm, he couldn't reach his dagger. The youngster continued to squirm, and it was all Titus could do to keep him pinned down.

"Get off me. Leave me alone," the boy said.

Hoofs clapped along the nearby dirt trail. Horses approached.

Titus leaned in tight so that he was nose to nose with the thief. "Shut up, boy," Titus whispered, but his eyes burned.

The boy stopped flailing, realizing both their lives were in danger.

The horses' steps slowed, but they were close. One steed snorted, followed by a man's voice. "I heard something."

"Eh, it's probably deer," a second man said.

"No, someone was talking."

Footfalls crunched the undergrowth and moved closer toward the camp.

"Come out and we won't hurt you," the voice said.

Titus and the boy continued to lock eyes, each wondering if they could trust the other. Both knew it was a better option than trusting the voice.

Bucktooth lifted its head, sensing the approaching danger. Titus could only pray that the animal wouldn't make a sound and give away their location.

The second voice called from the trail, "Come on. We need to reach camp and return to Marmaduke before morning, or he'll have our head."

Silence followed until the steps clopped back to the path and the horses left.

Titus kept all his weight on the boy with his eyes glued to him. "I'm not going to hurt you, okay?"

The boy nodded.

"I'm going to get off you. If you try to run or take anything, then I *will* hurt you."

The boy nodded again.

Titus eased his body off the boy, who rolled away and considered escape.

"Not a very good plan—sneaking around trying to steal from others." Titus huffed in the boy's direction, who kept swiveling his head, unable to decide if he wanted to run. His options were limited and poor. The trail might have more of Marmaduke's men and the forest had individuals more unsavory than himself.

"How old are you, anyway? Thirteen?"

This paused the boy. "I'm fifteen," he said, insulted.

Most thieves were older. Often, they were former soldiers who didn't have a war to fight.

"What are you doing out here?" Titus asked.

The question left the boy speechless. He gritted his teeth and pursed his lips. Even in the darkness, his face reddened with anger.

Titus pressed for a response. "I asked, what are you doing out here?"

"A soldier from Kensington's army was brought to our village. He was very sick. My father took him in. Marmaduke's men came a couple days later and found him." The boy paused as his jaw locked with emotion. After several breaths, he calmed himself. "They killed my family. I managed to escape."

The story should've triggered empathy, but Titus refused to engage. He had no interest in commiserating about their similar tragedies. Instead, Titus weighed the boy's words with suspicion. "Are you sure he was from Kensington's army? They are under siege in the castle."

"Maybe some are, but Kensington isn't there. I saw him."

Titus stroked his chin, weighing the new information. "Where is your village?"

"By Gardner Lake a few miles east."

Titus knew the area. In the early days during the war with the barons, Charles's forces didn't have a castle. They were a ragtag group who had to survive in the hills, and they chose Black Mountain, a craggy peak near Gardner Lake. The rock outcroppings provided plenty of safe places to hide.

"Can you show me the way to your village?"

"I'm never going back to my village."

"I'm not asking you to go to your village. I just need the way to it."

"Why? What are you going to do?" the boy asked.

"Not your business."

The boy glared at Titus. "Give me some of your food."

"Do you want to get a beating?"

"You can't catch me. I can tell you're injured."

Titus groused under his breath. The boy was smart. "I don't have much." He opened the satchel and pulled out a strip of meat and tore it in half.

The youngster may as well have been drooling as his eyes locked onto the food.

"Half now and half when we get where I need to go."

The boy nodded.

Titus tossed him a chunk. The boy sank his teeth into it and grunted with satisfaction.

"What's your name?"

The boy hesitated. "Michael. You?"

"Titus."

Michael chortled with mild amusement as he chewed. "Like the famous warrior."

"Yeah. Like the famous warrior."

CHAPTER 17

When people talked about the stories from the war with the barons, they spoke of the major battles. Few mentioned the beginning, when the rebellion was nothing more than a whisper in hushed conversations. During that period, Black Mountain served as the campsite for Charles and his band of men to recruit and strategize. Only the most loyal men were invited there, not that anyone would *want* to stay on the giant rock. The rugged peak left a lot to be desired, but with snaking trails, loblolly pines, and clusters of boulders, Black Mountain offered plenty of places to hide from the watchful eyes of the barons' spies. Fortunately, the uprising took root, so the time on the unforgiving terrain was brief. Only a handful of soldiers who'd been on the mountain were still alive. Kensington was not among them, but Harold was. Titus looked forward to seeing a familiar face and thanking his friend for saving his life. He began the day with a bounce in his step, even if it also included a limp.

Michael led the way off the trail and used physical features like a map to guide them. They followed a gully, then a stream, and finally Black Mountain emerged in the distance. The dark granite gave the feature its color and inspired its uncreative name. Though far from a gigantic summit, the eight thousand foot elevation to its peak tested most men's abilities.

During the trek, Titus alternated between riding and walking. His leg still wasn't strong enough to hike long distances, but it had improved.

When they reached the base of the mountain, Titus stopped. "All right. I'll go on from here." Titus opened the satchel and handed Michael the half strip of venison, as promised.

The boy took it, and Titus walked on ahead with the horse.

"Wait," Michael said. "Where are you going?"

"It's best for you not to know."

"Are you going to fight Marmaduke?" Michael asked.

Titus stopped in his tracks, but didn't turn around. He wanted to leave and forget he'd ever met Michael. The fewer people who knew about Black Mountain, the better, but he'd been right about one thing. The boy was smart. He turned toward Michael and exhaled with more than a hint of irritation.

"I'm going with you," Michael said.

"Says who?"

Michael's tough exterior cracked along with his voice. "I have nowhere to go. They killed my family."

Like Titus, Michael needed something—a purpose. Or maybe just a distraction. Titus grunted and continued hiking. "This way." He waved for Michael to follow, and they passed through a narrow crevice created by two massive rock slabs. The duo ascended further, and the incline forced Titus to stop often to rest. The day's march had caught up to him.

Giant boulders lay in further up the slope. Titus grimaced from fatigue and exasperation. *How much higher must they climb and would they find anyone?* As they neared the rocks, soldiers jumped out with swords drawn.

Michael cowered behind Titus, who didn't flinch.

The men stared at Titus and then glanced at one another in shock. *Was it Titus back from the dead?*

"It's me," Titus said. "And the boy is with me." He continued past the puzzled men, leading Michael and the horse. The soldiers' odd reaction left Michael scrutinizing Titus's appearance more closely. Titus could almost read the boy's thoughts. *Had he been traveling with the "legend" all this time? It couldn't be.* Titus could understand the boy's confusion. The stories of Titus versus his hobbled condition were irreconcilable.

As they navigated past the boulders, Titus expected Kensington and a swarm of enthusiastic soldiers to greet them, but instead, he found less than three dozen men with heads held low, gathered around a pathetic fire with flames no higher than a hand. Knut and Kensington were among them, along with Walter, the lesser noble he'd traded swords with. Besides that, Titus recognized a few faces, but didn't know their names.

Kensington stood when he saw Titus. The other men remained seated and barely raised their heads. Curiously, many wore scowls. Perhaps it was their less than ideal living situation, or maybe it was Titus's limp, but his return did not inspire them.

Kensington hurried over and pulled Titus aside. "It's good to see you."

"And you. Where's Harold?"

Kensington's jaw tightened. "He got sick. We took him to a villager, but Marmaduke's men found him and..." He didn't need to finish the sentence.

The news was like a gut punch that knocked the air out of Titus's lungs. Harold had been a good friend, one Titus took for granted, and now he was gone. Titus eyed Michael. Harold must have been the soldier Michael's father had taken in. The boy had buried his grief, but Kensington's comment brought it bubbling to the surface, causing his eyes to well up.

"Would you tie up the horse?" Titus offered the reins to Michael to give him something to do and leave him alone with Kensington. As soon as he was out of earshot, he focused on Kensington. "I'd heard you were at Fennelworth."

Kensington shook his head. "Some men made it there. I'm not sure how many. After the battle, Marmaduke's forces almost captured me twice, but I managed to find a few of the soldiers, including Harold. He told us the stories of Black Mountain, and we found others along the way."

"So what's the plan?" Titus asked.

Kensington stammered, "We continue to let people know the war isn't over. We… don't engage Marmaduke. Spring will be here soon. We must rebuild our forces and prepare as best we can."

The vague statements might placate a common soldier, but Titus saw through the generic comments. There was no plan.

"Is it true about Lord Chaucer and Gilroy?" Titus asked.

"Yes. And there's more," Kensington said.

"What?"

Kensington took a deep breath. "Before the battle of Kent, Marmaduke had gone to Baron Hughes."

The name triggered Titus. "The son of Baron Zaun?"

Baron Zaun was the most vile of the wicked barons and the last to fall in the great war. Titus met him on the field in his final stand. Zaun didn't last more than a few moments against Titus's ire.

Kensington nodded. "Marmaduke told him you were fighting. Hughes immediately turned over two hundred crossbowmen at no cost to avenge his father's death."

The revelation stunned Titus into silence. The crossbowmen were the reason they'd lost the battle, and maybe the war. He leaned against a rock in a stupor. Marmaduke had been thinking ten steps ahead. His son wasn't murdered in a random act of violence. In the seconds after Marmaduke had learned who Titus was, he'd seen the opportunity before him. If Titus would not join him, then he'd goad the "legend" into fighting for the other side and he'd gain support from the wicked barons' heirs. It was as clever as it was sadistic.

The realization left him filled with shame, even though he'd done nothing wrong. He glanced at the soldiers around the camp fire. The awkward peeks and scowls now made sense. It wasn't that they blamed him for losing, or maybe they did, but the men knew what had happened and why.

"Get something to eat," Kensington said. "When it's safe, we're going to push further north." He passed Titus and was about to pat him on his left shoulder, but thought better of it. "I'm glad you're alive."

Titus turned and shuffled over to the paltry food offering near the fire. No one made eye contact with him or spoke. Instead, they kept their heads buried. The chilly reception made Rosalind's barn feel toasty. Titus leaned down to the small pot filled with a watery porridge and a handful of hollowed out gourds that served as rudimentary cups. He took two and dipped them into the pot. Rather than invite Michael over, Titus wisely returned to the boy who sat by himself next to the makeshift stable, which was an alcove the men had been blocked off with three large tree branches. The enclosure contained over a dozen horses, including Bucktooth.

Titus handed Michael a cup. The boy's hunger prevented him from asking questions. Instead, he slurped the stew while Titus sipped, deep in thought. The day had begun with such promise, but things were worse than Titus could have imagined. The army, if he could call it that, was decimated and starving.

Titus's friend, Harold, had been killed, and he'd been used by Marmaduke like a pawn.

After Michael gulped the last drops from the gourd, he turned his attention to the men who sat with their backs to them. "Is this really all that's left of the army?" he whispered.

Titus didn't respond.

"What can they do against Marmaduke's army?" Michael asked.

Titus had the same question.

NIGHTTIME FELL across Black Mountain like a frigid blanket. Titus had almost forgotten the misery of the weather, but the gusts of icy wind reminded him of the harsh nights many years ago. It had gotten so cold, two men had even frozen to death. Titus could still remember their frost-covered bodies, one on each side of the camp like macabre statues. Each man squatted with his arms around his legs, head tucked between his knees. It also was the way Michael now sat.

Titus and Michael's location outside the stable left them exposed to the blustery flurries. If they were inside the alcove, they'd be warmer, but the horses might trample or kick them. Titus wanted to move closer to the soldiers and the fire, but given the circumstances, he didn't think the others would welcome him. He surveyed the area and noticed a slight indentation along one of the stone walls.

"Come with me," he said to Michael. Titus led the youngster to the nook. Three sides protected it from the elements. He motioned for Michael to lie down on the inside so that he faced the rock. Titus laid down so his back was against Michael's and he'd block any wind from reaching the boy.

After several minutes of silence, Michael whispered, "Are you the Titus from the legends?"

"You have eyes," Titus said, without either confirming or denying anything.

Gusts howled across the mountain, causing the men around the fire to shiver. Titus didn't bother trying to sleep, nor did he feel like it. He couldn't fathom how his life had ended up this way. There'd been so much pain and misery since his wife's death, and it only continued. His son's last words rattled in his head. *Why?*

Why had God forsaken him, and why would he allow someone like Marmaduke to win? Titus didn't fear death itself, but he was afraid of dying in a whimper. He was also afraid of Marmaduke being king and what he'd do to others. But mostly, Titus feared that his entire life and everyone in it would be rendered meaningless.

Titus remembered little after that. Maybe the wind died or his mind shut down, but he drifted asleep. When his eyes opened, dawn had broken. No one else was awake except Kensington, who sat alone on a rock, twirling the tip of his sword in the dirt.

No great revelation or epiphany came to Titus from his dreams, but he was certain about what he wouldn't do. If he was going to die, it would not be freezing or starving to death on this pile of rocks. He pulled himself to his feet and shuffled to Kensington.

"Good morning, Titus."

"And to you, my lord."

Kensington shook his head. "You don't need to call me that."

Titus nodded, appreciative of the gesture. "We need food, and I have an idea, but I need some men."

"Some men?" Kensington stopped twirling the sword.

"Titus, I didn't share everything with you the other day. I've heard whispers. Many are thinking about deserting. The only reason they haven't already is because it isn't safe. Marmaduke's soldiers still patrol the trails, and they've been checking the villages for survivors."

Titus chewed on that for a moment. "Then we remind the men what they are fighting for?"

The comment elicited a hollow smirk from Kensington. "What *are* they fighting for?"

"They fight to be ruled by a king worthy of the title."

Kensington raised a skeptical eyebrow. "Is that why you're fighting?"

Titus paused. "Marmaduke cannot be king."

Kensington did not miss the subtle difference. "I've always respected your honesty, Titus."

"Good, because I need you to release me from my word."

"What do you mean?"

"It's time for me to fight."

Kensington chortled. "Fight? You can barely hold a sword right now. We need to go north so we can survive."

"For what? So Marmaduke can march north in pursuit of us and murder anyone who doesn't follow him along the way?"

"Marmaduke has retreated to Doldren Castle for the winter. He split his forces. Most are with him. The rest lay siege to Fennelworth. If we go north, we can find a proper shelter for the winter. We don't have a chance here, Titus."

"Then we have nothing to lose."

"Just our lives," Kensington said. "And what could you possibly do with the number of soldiers we have?" He waved his hand toward the cluster of sleeping men.

"We have to try. Let me talk to them."

Kensington chuckled under his breath. "Titus, if you can get them to do anything, King Charles will turn over in his grave."

CHAPTER 18

A few soldiers stirred and sat upright when they found Titus standing in front of them, leaning against a rock. A few nudged others awake. Michael remained in his nook and watched from a distance.

"Good morning," Titus said.

The men didn't respond.

"Who is happy today?" Titus asked.

The men looked at each other. *Was Titus serious?*

"Who is happy about living like some rodent, hiding away in the hole of some mountain?"

No one answered, but no one needed to. Titus pushed himself off the rock and paced back and forth, avoiding hobbling as much as possible.

"Who is happy that Marmaduke is going to be king?" Titus stroked his chin. "Marmaduke believes he's already won. His men are dancing and singing in their camps, drunk with wine. They have nothing to fear." Titus stopped pacing and stared at the troops. "What if we gave them something to fear?"

A couple of soldiers stifled their laughter.

"We can't fight them," one of them groused.

"Yes, we can. We just don't fight the way they want us to."

The soldier waved away Titus's comment like it meant nothing.

"He's got too many knights," a man said.

"And too many archers and crossbowmen," a second added.

"And we know how that happened," someone muttered under their breath.

The remark brought a silence to the discussion and Titus resumed his pacing. "Yes, I heard the story. I'm also aware of how he recruited large portions of his army. I assume you all have heard *those* stories."

The men averted their eyes. Of course, they knew of the atrocities Marmaduke had committed.

"How do you think he'll rule as king?"

The men hung their heads. They didn't need to answer the rhetorical question.

"Is your plan to run today so you can die tomorrow?" Titus glared at Knut. At first, the big man stared back until Titus added, "How noble."

Knut dropped his gaze.

"I'm going to fight," Titus said. "And I'm not waiting for spring. I'm fighting today. If you want to fight, I'll be over there." He pointed to a rock beside Michael.

Titus ambled over and sat down. Michael side-eyed him and must've wondered if he was crazy. The men mumbled amongst themselves. Titus couldn't hear the details of what they said, but the response to his speech was not what he expected, but maybe it should've been.

No one came over.

TITUS HAD NEVER BEEN KNOWN for his oratory skills. That was another one of Charles's specialties. Titus led by example, and he hoped that his willingness to fight would bleed into the others, but all remained planted by the fire. He kept his eye on Knut, hoping he'd join. The men looked up to the big man, literally and figuratively. If he fought, others would follow, but Knut stared at the tiny flames without a flinch. The soldiers began whispering among themselves, and then they chatted as if Titus had never spoken.

Michael leaned over to Titus. "I will fight with you, even if you're not the real Titus."

The real Titus. That's when it sunk in. For years, people had viewed Titus as "the legend." They respected him and looked up to him without even knowing him. Without the aura, there was no relationship or goodwill to fall back on, as he'd made no effort to know the men. They only had the memory of a battle where Titus was supposed to be an asset to the army instead of its greatest liability.

"I will fight with you," Michael said again.

Titus looked Michael up and down. Sure, he was about Aidan's age and something reminded him of his son, but those qualities were ignored. Titus should've said, "No, it's too dangerous, Michael. You're barely a man," but Titus's paternal instincts had died when his son did. Instead, he focused on the boy's reason for fighting. Nothing would take away the pain of his family's slaughter, just like nothing would take away his own anguish. But there was retribution. They could at least try for that. "You know what could happen to you?" Titus asked to ensure the boy understood the stakes..

Michael nodded.

As they spoke, a man stood, and all five feet of him walked over. He was so small he was easy to miss, including the weapon slung over his shoulder, which fittingly was a short bow. Curly black hair hung over his sky-blue eyes, and a heavy beard covered the rest of his face. He passed through the other men, who tilted their heads and eyed him with curiosity.

When the little man reached Titus, he stroked his chin while studying Titus from head to toe. "You don't strike me as stupid."

"Thank you," Titus said, while knowing it wasn't a compliment.

"So I assume you're not planning to fight Marmaduke straight up."

"That is correct."

"Okay, then. I'm in," the man said.

The bluntness caught Titus off guard. "You want to fight?" He asked to make sure he'd heard the man correctly.

"Are you leaving the mountain?"

Titus nodded.

"Then, yes."

Titus furrowed his brow and suspected the man might be a few arrows short of a full quiver. "The reason you want to fight is that I'm leaving the mountain?"

"Yes, I don't like it here." The man showed no fear of what might happen off the mountain.

"What's your name?" Titus asked.

"Horace."

Titus pointed to the bow. "Are you good with that?"

"I better be. Look at me." Horace motioned to his less than intimidating frame.

Titus smirked. Horace might not be all there, but Titus had no alternative, and one archer might be enough for his plan. "Okay. Let's go."

As the trio passed Kensington, Titus whispered, "I'm borrowing the two best horses." He didn't wait for permission and entered the make-shift corral with the steeds, including Bucktooth. The old horse ambled over when he saw Titus.

"Don't worry, pal." Titus rubbed the animal's cheek. "You're off the hook." Titus pointed to a majestic brown stallion. "Horace, take that one." He then led Michael to a beautiful black mare and mounted the steed. He offered his good arm to Michael and hoisted him onto the rear of the saddle.

Titus kicked his heels into the animal's sides and the mare headed down the narrow trail. He glanced at the rest of the men, hoping others would join, but all the faces, including Kensington, watched with incredulous stares as if they were crazy.

Maybe they were right.

CHAPTER 19

After seven miles of riding, Horace pulled up alongside Titus and Michael and asked, "How are we going to attack Marmaduke with our army of three?"

"Does it matter? You're off the mountain," Titus said.

Horace arched an eyebrow. "Fair point."

Titus studied Horace, who looked off into the forest. He was a strange man, to be sure, but there was something about him that Titus liked. "Have you laid siege to a castle?" he asked.

Horace shook his head. "Can't say that I have."

"The focus is on the stronghold and trying to stop people from escaping."

Horace shrugged, unsure how that constituted a battle plan, but he continued riding and trusted Titus would share the details when he was ready. And he did. Their target was the supply wagon Titus had seen the day before. After Titus explained the scheme, Horace offered a simple nod while leaving Michael to ponder whether it was audacious or insane.

When the trio were within two miles of Fennelworth Castle, they dismounted and led the horses to a tree far off the trail.

They tied the reins to a branch and headed toward the main trail.

Before reaching the road, Titus stopped them. "You understand the plan, correct?"

Horace grunted, which Titus took as a 'yes.' Michael stared with fearful eyes in a silent stupor.

"Horace takes out the knight closest to him with a surprise arrow." Titus pointed to Michael. "All you need to do is scream and make a bunch of noise like it's an ambush. The second man will get spooked and ride away."

Titus turned to Horace and spoke slowly. "If there are more than two, don't shoot." He stared back at Michael. "Just leave. Understood?"

Both nodded.

Titus hobbled onto the trail's edge and waited. Horace and Michael hid, one on each side. As Titus remained in the open, he couldn't hide from the fact that his plan had several holes, but he didn't share them with Michael or Horace. He rationalized the omission by taking the riskiest assignment. His plan was also the best he could come up with based on the information and limited men.

An hour passed.

Titus sat down to rest his leg. After another hour, Titus considered abandoning the plan altogether. But then the ground trembled.

Titus pulled himself to his feet. The earth shook as hoof beats thundered closer. Titus faced the direction they were coming, and in seconds, two knights rode toward him, pulling a wagon of supplies. It was the same duo he'd seen before. He held up his hand for the soldiers to stop.

The knights yanked their reins and slowed the horses. Titus's heart raced, but he concealed his nerves. Everything was going according to plan. This could actually work, but then, a third knight rode up. Titus pursed his lips and considered running, but his injured leg would make an escape next to impossible. When a fourth man emerged, Titus's jaw clenched and his stomach churned. His simple plan could've succeeded, but with four soldiers, there was no chance of scaring anyone, which was the reason he ordered Horace and Michael to leave if there were more than two.

The knights sized up Titus. In his plain tunic, he didn't pose a threat, but these men were not fools. They surveyed the area for danger.

"Out of the way, old man," the first knight said.

"My crops failed," Titus said in as meek of a voice as possible. "I don't have enough to survive winter. Can you help me?"

"We have nothing for you. Now move."

Titus bowed and limped aside, which caught the attention of the third knight, who dismounted and approached. "Are you injured?"

"My knee twisted while working."

The soldier stood in front of Titus and studied every inch of him. "Who are you and where do you live, old man?"

Titus's heart raced faster. He didn't want to reveal his name, and he didn't want to say a location they knew was a lie. "I am a peasant who works the land. My home is a few miles away, near Miller Creek."

"A few miles? That's more like ten. Where's your horse?"

"I walked." As soon as he said it, he knew he'd been backed into a lie.

"On a twisted knee?" The knight unsheathed his sword.

Titus considered reaching for the dagger hidden under his hem, but he doubted he could reach it and surprise the knight. "It's been a long and arduous journey," Titus said.

"Let's see this injured knee. Lift your tunic," the knight said.

If he saw Titus's actual injury, he'd know Titus was lying. A fight was imminent. Even if he snuck a dagger past the knight's defenses, it would still be three against one.

Pffft.

An arrow zinged out of the trees, tagged the first knight on horseback, and lodged in his chest. The second soldier shouted, "We're under attack!"

The knight in front of Titus turned to assess the danger. Titus pulled the dagger and thrust it into his neck. The soldier tried to ram his sword forward, but Titus jerked him close and fell down on top of him as the man bled out.

Michael rustled the leaves in the forest and shouted. Horace stepped out from the opposite side and took aim with another arrow. The missile sailed and tagged the third knight in the neck, piercing it all the way through. The remaining knight released the carriage and spurred his horse.

Horace remained focused, pulled a third arrow, aimed, and let it fly. It whipped through the air and struck the knight in the back, causing him to tumble off the horse.

Titus shoved the dead man off him and stood. Michael and Horace stepped out onto the trail. All three sucked wind from the brief but intense encounter.

Titus turned to Horace. "I said no shooting if there were more than two."

"If I shot two, there wouldn't be," Horace said, as if his answer made perfect sense.

Titus didn't bother arguing and nodded in gratitude.

Before the fight, Titus had expected one knight would escape in a best case, so they would've needed to grab what they could and flee the area as quickly as possible. The fact they took out all the knights meant they were no longer rushed. They used one of the knight's horses to tug the carriage off the trail and hide it in the trees. Then, they dragged away all the bodies and covered them with branches and leaves.

Once they finished, the trio inspected the spoils and discovered four burlap sacks filled with bread rolls. Two more contained salted meat. The biggest prize was the wine—seven rundlets and three smaller wine skins. They didn't dare pull the wagon back through the uneven terrain. Instead, Titus brought the horses over and loaded up three with as much as they could carry. He jerry-rigged the saddles so two rundlets hung off a horse, one on each side, to balance it out. Given the volume of food and odd number of rundlets, they left the last one in the wagon.

Titus led the caravan of six steeds through the forest, away from the main trail. This resulted in a return journey that was twice as long, and when they reached Black Mountain, it was dark.

The exhausted trio passed through the narrow crevice between the giant boulders and found the men huddled together even more depressed than before. When the first man caught sight of them, he elbowed the two beside him. Others stirred and turned around. Jaws dropped and several men pointed at the horses packed with wine. The looks on their faces made it all worth it.

"Who's hungry?" Titus asked.

The troops swarmed the entourage and pulled the sacks of bread and meat off. Others grabbed the wine and popped a spigot as fast as they could. One man held his head in shock. "How did you do this?"

"Horace and Michael did it." Titus smiled at the two and the other men shouted their names.

Kensington walked over and Titus handed him a wine skin. "For the king."

The men cheered for Kensington.

For the rest of the night, the soldiers felt like men again as they ate and drank while being regaled with the story of the assault. Kensington regained his bravado and spoke as if he'd helped with the daring plan. Titus didn't bother correcting him. The men needed to believe in the king. Everyone except for Knut relaxed and enjoyed the moment. He sat off to the side, sipping a gourd full of wine without talking to anyone.

Titus leaned over to Kensington. "What's wrong with Knut?"

"He still wants his title. Doesn't seem likely given the current state of affairs."

"You think he'll leave?" Titus asked.

Kensington shrugged. It was a strong possibility.

"He's your best warrior."

"Present company excluded, of course." Kensington patted Titus on the shoulder, the wine perhaps having an effect. Titus eyed Kensington, who removed his hand and regained his composure. "If he thinks we can win," Kensington said, "then he might stay. If not, he will pursue other options."

The precarious situation with Knut reminded Titus that while they had a glimmer of hope, it was only just that.

CHAPTER 20

Titus woke early, plagued by a myriad of questions that refused to let him rest. Despite the unexpected food and drink, a giant question still loomed. How could they win a war against Marmaduke? If the men didn't believe it was at least a possibility, then it was only a matter of time before they deserted. But how could they win? They needed more soldiers and food, and there were no promising leads for either. The supplies Titus had stolen might last a week, and it wasn't like they could keep raiding caravans. No doubt, word would get back to Marmaduke about the missing supply wagon. Maybe he'd conclude that a few of his conscripts made off with the booty, but regardless, he would send future carriages with more than a four knight escort. If Titus tried another ambush, they'd end up in a skirmish, and Marmaduke would hope to make it a full scale battle. Marmaduke also might lay a trap. Given how crafty he'd been, it was possible he'd place spies in the forest who would follow them to Black Mountain. If that happened, they'd be wiped out in a day.

As the sun illuminated the site, men stirred and awakened

with glum faces. They no longer had the comfort of a deep alcohol induced sleep or the illusion of their dreams. Instead, the harsh reality of their situation greeted them, which was only modestly better on a full stomach. Should they desert their king, a crime punishable by death? Although it might be a hollow threat given the circumstances, the offense still carried a heavy stigma. And even if they fled, their subsequent prospects remained poor. If they absconded in groups, they'd be easier to find by Marmaduke's troops. On top of that, no village would accept a party of wandering men. They'd be viewed as bandits or thieves. If they went solo, each man would have to face the dangers of the forest alone and they'd be at the mercy of others. Ultimately, they'd need a noble to take them in. If anyone discovered the dishonor of their desertion, they still might be killed. In every scenario, their futures were bleak.

The only person with a brighter outlook was Knut. His family had ties to the northeast, and given the ever changing political landscape, he might have better luck finding a noble who'd take him in because his father's name still carried some weight. His size and fighting prowess would also make him an asset. If the big man fled, as Kensington suspected, others would follow, and the small army would collapse in days.

As each man wrestled with the decision of staying or deserting, they avoided eye contact and many kept their heads buried between their knees. Titus wanted to say something to lift their spirits, but after his last speech failed, he hesitated.

Kensington also sensed the men needed motivation, so he walked in front to address the group. "Good morning, my loyal brethren." He spoke with a positive energy that belied their predicament. Perhaps the food had gone to his head or, more likely, Kensington realized this was his last gasp to keep the army together.

The men sat up and listened to their king, eager for a distraction.

"I trust everyone feels more refreshed after a good meal," Kensington said. "We're grateful to Titus, Horace, and Michael for the provisions they've provided. It will help as we rebuild the army."

"How are we going to do that?" a soldier asked.

With a spry smile and dramatic hand gestures, Kensington explained, "We're going to rally. We're going to expand our recruitment territory. We're going to increase the size of our forces and we're going to strategize how to retake our land." He clenched his fist for emphasis and finished with a smirk, as if he knew all the details.

"How?" one soldier asked.

Kensington's energetic veneer cracked. The silence that followed was only a couple of seconds, but if crickets lived on Black Mountain, they would've been chirping for all to hear.

Titus didn't have time to think of the perfect thing to say. He had to act before any remaining will of the men bled out, so he coughed and limped over. All eyes bore up at him until he stood beside Kensington. Titus stared back at the troops with an unflinching gaze. Now all he needed was something smart to say. Something clever. Something inspiring.

"We end the siege." The words fell out of Titus's mouth, and a few chuckled, not because it was funny, but because of how ridiculous it sounded. Even Kensington stared at Titus, confused.

No turning back now, so Titus continued, "Our men are in that castle. They're waiting to fight. They don't know we're out here ready to help them. If we attack from the rear, we can engage the enemy on two fronts and win." Titus wasn't sure how he came up with the idea. It just happened. The only immediate source of warriors was Fennelworth, and somehow, someway, they needed to get them.

"We don't even know how many people are in the castle," a soldier said.

"And how will they know when to attack?" another asked.

These were reasonable questions, and Titus didn't have the answers. He needed more time and more information. He also required Kensington's help, but the inexperienced king stared at Titus like a lost puppy. It was a look Titus had seen before when Kensington was younger, and most recently during the battle of Kent.

Stunned jaws hung open. The men weren't ready to fight, and Titus couldn't blame them after what happened at Kent. Rather than attempting to convince them, he tried a different approach. "What do *you* think we should do?" He pointed to the group.

Silence followed until one soldier said, "We need to get a message to the people inside."

Titus nodded. "What else?"

Another man replied, "We need to know how many we'd have to fight. So we know if we have a chance."

Titus nodded again. If men thought there was a chance, that was progress. "Okay," Titus said. "I will scout the castle. I will get a message inside, and when I come back, I will share the battle plan. You can all decide then if you're willing to fight. Fair enough?"

The men remained seated, and no one flinched or spoke. Sweat filled Titus's palms, despite the chilly weather. This had gone as well as his last speech.

Kensington stepped in front of Titus. "Of course it is. And my brave warriors will fight against the tyranny," he said in a deep, regal voice while nodding in encouragement.

One by one, the men bobbed their heads, except for Knut, who remained in the back with a stone-faced expression.

"Who can write?" Titus asked.

Several individuals raised their hands. Titus waved over the man closest to him. "Find something to write on and something to write with." He passed through the seated men in front and when he reached Knut, he paused. "Knut, would you help me with the horse?"

The big man growled under his breath, but walked with Titus to the stable and out of earshot.

"You've been awfully quiet, Knut."

Knut stared at the ground. He'd already checked out.

"What is it you want?" Titus asked.

Knut pursed his lips at the ridiculous question. "To restore my family's honor."

In moments like these, those in charge made promises. Some they intended to keep. Some they didn't. A few they couldn't. Regardless, the objective was simple. Do and say whatever was necessary to win. Titus hated these situations and refused to promise something he couldn't guarantee.

"What happened the last time your family fled?" Titus asked.

Knut didn't answer.

"Will you honor your father if you lose your baronet title?"

Knut huffed. "Baronet." Derision dripped from his lips. "It's like saying little baron. Even if I cared for that worthless title, what good does it do if I'm dead?"

"Being dead must certainly be better than being a lesser noble," Titus said with a biting sarcasm that matched Knut's disdain.

"I could also be captured and sold into slavery," Knut replied, unaffected by Titus's attempt to play to his conscience.

"These are not my lands. The people only respect me because I can fight. A title and land are the only way I can change that."

"If that's all you seek, then staying is your best option. I was around with King Charles after the war. I saw who he rewarded. Those who fought when things were darkest received the best titles and the best lands. Look." He gestured to the small army. "There's barely anyone left for Kensington."

Knut raised an intrigued eyebrow. "What happened to your title and land?"

"I declined the king's offer."

"Why?"

Titus shook his head. "Doesn't matter. If that's what you seek, that's what you'll get."

"If we win," Knut clarified.

"At least wait to hear the plan."

Knut didn't respond. Not a good sign.

Titus entered the stable to find a horse for the day while Knut returned to the men. Michael stepped toward the animals. "Can I go with you?"

"Not this time."

Michael glanced over at the other soldiers like an outsider.

"You'll be fine, Michael," Titus said. "You helped get them their wine." Titus led a stallion out of the stable and stopped next to Horace. "Can I borrow your bow?"

"Why don't you just ask to sleep with my wife?"

"Didn't know you were married," Titus said.

"I'm not. Just need you to understand what you're asking for," Horace said.

"I need to launch a message over the castle walls."

"Okay," Horace said, but he didn't hand over his bow. He went to the alcove and found a horse of his own.

Titus didn't argue. Instead, he told the soldier who could write the details of the note, who transcribed the information onto a piece of deerskin. Once it was done, Titus stuffed it into his pocket, along with a thin strip of leather.

Titus walked next to Kensington, leaned toward his ear, and whispered, "Don't let Knut leave."

Kensington offered a stern nod. "No one leaves."

Titus grabbed the reins of his horse and left the camp with Horace. As they rode down the mountain, Titus wondered whether Kensington had the tougher of the two assignments. Of course, if Titus failed, he'd be killed.

CHAPTER 21

The duo rode through the forest, off the main path. The plodding pace gave ample time for Titus to think. His plan sounded easy—launch an arrow over the castle's wall with a message wrapped around its shaft. Unfortunately, measures would be in place to prevent such a scheme. Messages like the one Titus carried had to be intercepted or the defenders would know when reinforcements would arrive. Laying siege was as much psychological as it was physical. The attackers needed those in the castle to believe it was hopeless to resist. Their choices were to starve, fight a battle they had no way of winning, or surrender and hope for mercy. Only one of those options had a chance of survival. For the mental warfare to be effective, the besiegers had to maintain a defensive perimeter that prevented anyone or anything from entering or leaving the stronghold.

As Titus wondered what defenses they'd encounter, Horace's head kept swiveling to and fro every time something made a noise. A hawk screeched deep in the woods and Horace turned left. A squirrel scampered up the side of a giant oak, its claws clattering against the bark, and Horace's eyes targeted right.

Titus had the same habit of always being on alert, a leftover instinct from the war. "Did you serve in King Charles's court?" Titus asked.

Horace shook his head.

"Did you fight in other battles? Before this?"

Horace grunted, which sounded like a "no."

"Then how did you end up in Kensington's army?"

"My home is further north. King Charles never expanded his hunting territory. Kensington said he would carry on King Charles's ways."

"You risk your life because of hunting?"

Horace's eyes widened, surprised Titus would even ask such a question.

Titus held up an apologetic hand, and the two continued through the forest, guiding their horses between the timbers. As they moved around a thicket of fir trees, the cicadas behind them stopped buzzing, which sent a shiver down Titus's spine that settled in the pit of his stomach. During the war with the barons, he'd learned to trust his gut, something that had served him well. Right now, his gut told him something or someone was lurking. He turned and studied the branches.

"What is it?" Horace asked.

Titus continued surveying the gaps between the leaves, fearful it was a Marmaduke spy. Nothing stood out. "Let's keep going."

They resumed riding, but every so often, Titus turned and checked if they were being followed. After the fifth time without finding anything, he gritted his teeth, frustrated. Perhaps he was rusty or just paranoid. Titus kicked the sides of his horse and they continued their journey.

When dusk was upon them, Titus and Horace hitched the horses to a tree a mile from Fennelworth. They couldn't take the chance that an unexpected neigh or snort from a horse would give away their position.

The main trail was sure to be guarded, so they stayed far off it, and moved through the shadows like ghosts. Enemy campfires in the distance served as beacons that guided them the rest of the way, but as they got closer, Titus cursed under his breath. A besieging army usually pitched simple tents for resting soldiers, but Marmaduke's forces had built a palisade around the camp. Titus had intended to return with the men from Black Mountain and ambush the sleeping troops, but the wooden walls ruined that idea. Worse still, as they crept closer, a more immediate issue materialized.

The campfires in the distance were actually giant bonfires in the middle of the open space separating the forest from Fennelworth. He'd forgotten about the clearing, a defensive measure *for* the castle. It aided the castle's archers and prevented enemy soldiers from sneaking up to the walls undetected. Unfortunately for Titus, the flames illuminated large swaths, making it unlikely that anyone could approach Fennelworth's walls without being seen. The only positive with their situation was they didn't need to reach the wall. They just had to get close enough for Horace to fire an arrow over it.

Titus pointed Horace to the darkest section of the forest next to the clearing. Thick bushes covered the ground, and branches from different trees intersected, making it impossible to know where one ended and the next began. Impatience and nerves tempted them to go faster, but they maintained a slow and steady pace. One slip or twig cracking underfoot would give them away.

When they finally reached the edge of the clearing, Titus

got a good look at their dilemma. The bonfires burned thirty yards into the hundred yard open space and they were separated forty yards apart. Each fire created a circle of light that almost formed a glowing ring around the castle.

"Can you launch the arrow from here?" Titus asked.

Horace shook his head. "The clearing is too big."

"Then we need to get you closer." Titus counted twelve sentry units around the perimeter and two near the palisade. Each group comprised five men, and they were well within shouting distance of each other. Titus and Horace were hidden between two of the units, with each about twenty-five yards away.

Sneaking up to a unit of that size undetected was unlikely, and it was even less likely that all the soldiers could be killed simultaneously. If they were lucky enough to pull that off, there were eleven other groups waiting to alert the sleeping garrison in the protected fort.

One ray of hope was the weather. The bitter cold forced the guards to huddle near tiny campfires at the clearing's edge. They stared at the flames, chatting and telling jokes to pass the time.

Titus pulled the deerskin message from his pocket and took one of Horace's arrows. He rolled the note around the shaft and tied it with the strip of leather. "Go out a few paces." Titus pointed to the shadows that extended into the clearing.

Horace grabbed the arrow and nudged himself out just enough to avoid the canopy of branches above.

"A little more," Titus whispered.

Horace edged out another couple of feet.

"More."

Horace glanced back, skeptical. He was completely exposed.

Titus waved him forward. They only had one shot.

Horace took a deep breath and then slithered out further. In a squatting position, he drew the bow back with all of his strength before releasing. The arrow whizzed through the air, arcing high into the night sky. It happened so fast, Titus lost sight of it.

Horace slinked back.

"Did it make it?" Titus asked.

Horace shook his head. "No. It glanced off the wall."

Titus's head slumped. "Then we have to wait until it's darker."

"And then what?" Horace asked.

"I'll sneak up to the wall and get the message." Titus searched the ground for a rock. "I'll tie the deerskin to this rock and throw it over."

Horace looked at the clearing and then at Titus. His eyes squinted with doubt.

"Do you have a better idea?" Titus asked.

"No, but we can't wait too long," Horace said. "Morning waits for no man."

Horace was right. They didn't have the luxury of time and returning to Black Mountain after failing would end the war in a whimper. But Titus also couldn't rush the attempt, as there were no second chances. He studied the bonfires, hoping they would run out of fuel, but the besiegers had staked large wooden planks in the ground that served as shields, which allowed the men to stoke the fire periodically with fresh logs.

Titus hoped to catch a unit during the later part of a shift when soldiers were tired and the bonfires as small as possible. Guards typically rotated in four-hour shifts, but he didn't know when the shift started, so he had to guess.

Titus rubbed his injured leg to get the blood flowing. If anyone saw him sneaking up to the wall, he'd have to run, something he'd not done since his injury. As he considered his long odds, the unsettled feeling from earlier in the day returned. Titus turned toward the forest and stared into the blackness.

Horace nocked an arrow and raised his bow. "What is it?" he whispered.

"Someone is out there."

CHAPTER 22

Both men stared at the wall of black, their eyes straining to see anything. Titus's muscles tensed, prepared to fight, and Horace kept his bow at the ready.

"Don't shoot," a quiet voice muttered.

Michael crawled out from the shadows. Titus was both relieved and angry. "Have you been following us this whole time?"

Michael stared at the ground.

"Why would you do that?" Titus asked.

Michael lifted his gaze and met Titus's eyes. "I want to help."

Titus shook his head. "Not for this."

"Why not? You're scouting."

Titus shrugged. "Yeah?"

"That's sneaking. It's what I'm good at."

"Apparently not that good."

Michael huffed. "I've been watching you this whole time."

Titus's jaw tightened. "There's nothing to do right now, anyway."

"Let me get the arrow." Michael motioned toward the castle wall.

Titus shook his head. "It's too dangerous."

"You think you have a better chance with that leg?" Michael eyed Titus's leg.

"I said, it's too dangerous."

"Look at that little bush." Michael pointed to the clearing. "And then that rock. Then that little rut. From there, I'm past the bonfires. It's darker and easier."

Titus stared. His old eyes noticed shadows, no bigger than a jug of ale. They were too small to hide behind. Titus shook his head. "No. We wait and then *I'll* sneak out to the wall."

Titus turned his attention to the guard units closest to him, shutting down any further discussion with Michael. For the next twenty minutes, he reassessed when to make a run for it. All the while, Horace fiddled with his bow, beyond bored, while Michael stared at the clearing. Finally, Titus rose to his feet and bent his knees like he was ready to run. "Alright, it's time."

Horace sat up, checked both units and then looked at Titus, curious if he was really going to do it.

Titus took three deep breaths. On the third, the soldiers' chatter quieted as if they knew the tension of the moment. Horace and Titus crouched lower and surveyed the unit to make sure they'd not been discovered. A commander from the garrison had approached and caught the group fooling around. A tongue lashing followed, leaving the men on edge. The units nearby heard the exchange and refocused their attention on their duty. Making a run for it now was suicide.

Titus met Horace's gaze. Without speaking, both knew the mission was over. When they turned, Michael was gone. They scanned the immediate area, but he was nowhere to be found.

Horace tapped Titus's shoulder and pointed to the small bush in the clearing.

"I'll be damned," Titus said.

Michael had contorted his body so that only a part of his foot extended out. He'd used the distraction of the garrison commander to make a run for it. His head peered out and when he deemed it safe, he slithered along the ground to the even smaller rock.

Titus shook his head in disbelief. No guard could tell the stone was slightly bigger than before, and Michael's movements were so smooth and low, someone would need to be staring right at him to notice. When Michael reached the rut, he had disappeared.

"I think the kid is better at sneaking than you," Horace said, his gaze glued to the clearing.

Titus didn't argue, but remained on edge. The boy still needed to deliver the message and return.

An hour passed and there was no sign of Michael. New guards swapped in and replaced the prior ones. Titus chewed his lip. The unit would be fresher and more attentive.

If someone spotted Michael near the castle, it would become a chase. If that happened, Titus knew he'd be the slowest. He leaned over to Horace. "If anything goes wrong, don't wait for me. Run with Michael and get away."

Horace offered no objection.

The two men held their position, staring at the shadows along the dark castle walls, hoping for any sign of the boy. Horace pointed to the clearing. Titus strained his eyes. Michael had already made it back to the small rock.

The guards nearby chatted amongst themselves and appeared none the wiser.

Michael crept to the bush and then returned to the forest.

"What took you so long?" Titus asked.

"I had to find the arrow," Michael said. "And then I needed to find a stone."

Titus motioned to the castle. "Did you do it? Is it over the wall?"

"Yes."

Horace playfully shoved Michael for a job well done.

Despite Titus's relief, he was still angry at Michael for disobeying him. "Alright, then. Let's get out of here."

TITUS, Michael, and Horace hiked during the final hours before dawn with heavy footsteps and heavier eyes. They found their horses and rode back half asleep. Titus wanted to curl up under a tree, but he refused to give in to the temptation. They still needed to reach Black Mountain and rally the men to fight.

Titus would face tough questions. Was the message read? He didn't know. How many soldiers were inside the castle and were they willing to fight? He didn't know that either. And finally, how would they defeat the protected garrison?

The sun cracked above the horizon and Black Mountain came into view. Michael and Horace smiled at one another. They'd made it.

When the horses reached the mountain's base, they sensed the end of the journey and quickened their pace. The animals huffed and snorted, eager to be reunited with their friends in the makeshift stable. The group passed through the giant boulders, but no guards emerged to greet them. Titus dismounted and walked further up the mountain. When he came around the giant rocks, his jaw dropped and his legs buckled.

The camp was empty.

CHAPTER 23

Titus dropped to a knee and felt the black ash where the fire had once burned. Cold. Very cold. The men had deserted long ago. Maybe they'd fled as soon as he'd left. The betrayal hurt. Titus had suffered many painful injuries in battle, including the two recent ones, but this pain was different. The physical sensation made sense. It could be explained. This injury couldn't and left him empty inside.

Horace led the horses into the alcove. The animals, though happy to rest, snorted in protest at the absence of their equine friends.

Michael scoured the area as if he'd find the men hiding somewhere. "I don't understand. Where did they go?"

Titus leaned against the rock wall and his shoulders slumped. All of their efforts had been for nothing.

Footsteps scraped along the rocks and dirt leading to camp. Titus pulled out his dagger and Horace nocked an arrow in his bow.

Walter sauntered into the space with his head down and his giant, jeweled sword sheathed in a scabbard. He jerked backward when he saw the trio. "You're back."

"Where is everyone?" Titus asked.

"Knut had us search the mountain for a better location since this one gets so cold at night. He sent one of us over here every few hours. Come with me." Walter waved them over.

Titus wanted to pull Walter in for a giant bear hug, his faith in humanity restored, until he considered the response again. "You said, Knut. Where's Kensington?"

"Kensington took a small contingent north to bring more people back from the Forani so we can expand our forces."

"Did he?" Titus said without revealing his simmering anger. Kensington probably fled to avoid future battles while the rest of his men stayed to fight for *his* kingdom. "What else did he say?"

"He said he had faith that you would end the siege. He would secure alliances with the Forani because a joint army with the Forani would be larger than Marmaduke's."

Titus gritted his teeth rather than say what he thought. The Forani were a hearty group of hunters who could survive in the most rugged conditions, but they weren't warriors, and there was no guarantee Kensington could deliver on such a promise. Titus wished more than anything that he could somehow smack Kensington. This was the type of thing he'd done in the prior war. He always remained in the rearguard while everyone else did the bloodiest fighting. How could he do that now? As king? But Titus couldn't challenge Kensington in front of Walter or anyone else, or he'd break what little morale existed.

"Lead us to the men," Titus said.

Walter led the group, including the horses, out of the alcove. They snaked through a winding trail until they passed a wide ravine that housed the other steeds. Titus guided the animals in, who neighed, eager to be reunited with their friends. The men continued on and the space opened into a much nicer area. It was like a cave except with a partially open ceiling. A large fire crackled in the middle and the remaining rations had been placed on a nearby rock. Everything about the place looked and felt like a real camp. Titus searched the faces, but Knut was nowhere to be seen until a grunt came from behind.

Titus turned and found the big man carrying armfuls of firewood.

"You were right," Knut said.

"About what?" Titus asked.

"About staying. I'm now the *Duke* of Cumberland," Knut said with pride.

"What an honor," Titus deadpanned.

Titus's dry response did nothing to change Knut's feelings. He carried the wood to an already impressive stack.

Titus could only guess at what other promises Kensington had made before leaving, and though relieved the army hadn't deserted, he knew the situation remained precarious. The men would expect details and a plan. He possessed neither.

WITHIN SECONDS, the men closed in on Titus, trapping him against the wall. His head whipsawed as they barraged him with questions.

"How many of Marmaduke's soldiers are there?"

"How many men are in the castle?"

"Were you able to talk to our people?"

"Who's there?"

There were others, but they all melded together. Titus took a deep breath. If he answered with the bitter truth, no one would fight, but he also didn't want to lie. During the war with the barons, Titus had listened to Charles give rallying speeches that were almost complete fabrications. Once, and in private, Titus called Charles out on his exaggerations. Titus never forgot

Charles's response. "If the lie is necessary for the greater good, it isn't a lie." After that, Titus could never trust Charles's word.

But now, as Titus wore the leadership shoes, he at least understood the dilemma Charles faced. Lying made sense. The soldiers staring at Titus needed guidance and inspiration. They didn't need the depressing truth.

Titus held up his hands and gestured with a pushing motion. "Back up and sit. I'll tell you everything I know."

The men complied. Titus walked towards the fire and waved for them to gather. The entire time, his mind raced. What would he say? Once everyone was seated, one soldier shouted, "How many of Marmaduke's men are there?"

While Titus didn't know the exact number, he had a solid estimate since he'd counted the sentry units and knew roughly how often they cycled in and out. He also could approximate how many tents could fit inside the palisade. "There are about three hundred."

Audible gasps and huffs echoed off the walls. The meeting was not off to a good start.

"Did you deliver the message?" another soldier asked.

Titus pointed at the man, eager to answer. "Yes. Yes, we did." He smiled to drive home the positive result. "Actually, Michael delivered the message." He waved back toward Michael, who stood along the back wall. It was the closest to a compliment that Titus would muster.

The boy's face turned red as several men turned around and offered nods of respect and appreciation.

"How many men are in the castle?" a soldier shouted.

"We don't know," Titus said.

More gasps, grunts of disapproval, and mutterings like "What are we going to do?" and "This isn't a plan."

Before the grumblings grew louder, Titus bellowed, "We will attack in three days."

The murmurs and complaining stopped, replaced by silence. All the men's eyes widened, and several mouths hung open in shock. After an extended period of awkward silence, the soldiers resumed grousing among themselves, and although Titus couldn't hear everything, he heard words like, "North," "No chance," and "It's over."

It was a make or break moment. The modest army was on the verge of collapse. Titus raised his voice again and commanded their attention. "Not counting the battle, raise your hand if you know someone that Marmaduke's men have killed?"

The men quieted as they considered the question.

Titus pressed for a response. "Who's lost a friend?"

Several men raised their hands.

"A neighbor?"

More hands raised.

"A family member?"

More arms went up. At this point, over half the men held a hand in the air.

"Who is hoping they have a friend in the castle?" Titus asked.

Everyone else raised their hands.

"What will Marmaduke do if we don't save them?"

No one needed to answer the rhetorical question. Everyone had heard the stories of Marmaduke's brutality, especially against anyone that opposed him.

A grizzled man standing in the back said what everyone thought, "But it's suicide if we attack them. Look at us."

"What's your name, soldier?"

The query caught the man off guard. "Randolph," he muttered.

"Randolph, I want to be clear about one thing. I'm not planning on dying and I don't want anyone else to. I made a

146

promise to myself about what I'm going to do in this war, and I intend to make good on that." A small sparkle of the legendary Titus shone through. "We *can* end the siege. We *can* save those men."

A few men shouted in support. It seemed the tide had turned in Titus's favor, but Knut brought them back to reality with one word.

"How?"

It was a fair question—a simple one, too. "I will reveal the strategy the day before the attack," Titus said. "Until then, rest and eat."

He needed the time to figure out an answer.

CHAPTER 24

Titus had heard stories about ancient generals defeating armies with numerical superiority, but he didn't know of one with a ten to one disadvantage. The famous Carthaginian general, Hannibal, defeated a massive army of almost one hundred thousand Romans with a force half the size. He won by enveloping the packed enemy, so they were squeezed together, making the horde of foot soldiers useless. Titus needed a clever strategy like that, but with his limited manpower, he couldn't envelop anyone. He had ten archers, five knights, and fifteen infantry. Thirty men. That was it. The besiegers' perimeter units alone had twice as many individuals. Within the palisade's walls, Titus estimated there were at least two hundred more.

Titus sat by himself, thinking. Anyone who glanced over may have assumed he was resting, but his mind toiled away, playing out battle scenarios. All ended with crushing defeats. Only an act of God could deliver a victory.

While Titus struggled alone, the men enjoyed the last of the bread and wine. "Anymore?" A soldier held a hollowed-out gourd under a spigot and tilted the rundlet to get the final few drops. Heads shook. No more.

"There's one more in the wagon we hid in the forest. We couldn't carry it all back," Michael said.

The words caught Titus's attention. The wagon might help them get closer to the enemy camp. He worked through the idea until the pieces of a daring plan coalesced. Maybe it could work. It was a long shot, but it had a chance. At least, he thought so. Titus had to share the scheme with one person— Horace. If he didn't agree, the rest didn't matter because of what he needed Horace to do. Titus waved him over. Horace knelt down beside Titus, who whispered to him. Horace listened, and then sat stone faced, offering no reaction.

"Horace?" Titus asked.

Horace remained silent.

"If you think it's too dangerous, you don't have to—,"

Without making eye contact, Horace interrupted, "I'm in." He didn't ask questions or suggest any changes, so Titus simply offered a nod of gratitude. Hopefully, everyone else would be so amenable.

The evening before the attack, Titus gathered the soldiers. The men sat in a circle around "the legend," their eyes glued to him. What genius tactics had he come up with?

Titus stood tall and tried to project an aura of confidence. "Men, I wouldn't ask you to do something that I wouldn't do myself. Horace and I will take the lead in the first attack. If we're not successful, then you do *not* need to attack, but if it works, we *will* win."

As Titus explained the risky plan, the men became more heartened by their chances, but it meant nothing unless Knut bought in. If he rejected it, others would, and Titus needed every last man, or failure was guaranteed. Knut had remained standing with his arms crossed the entire time. When Titus finished speaking, he looked at Knut, who stared back before offering a single small nod.

They now had a chance. Titus's plan *could* work; however, success hinged on many factors, including one giant unknown —the men from the castle had to fight.

———

THE NEXT EVENING, Titus hitched his stallion to the supply wagon that they'd stashed in the forest after their raid. Titus never thought he'd need it again or the leather armor from one of the corpses, but both were essential. He slipped the protective gear on, mounted his horse, and pulled the cart to the trail. Horace hid in the wagon bed with a blanket covering him. There was also the rundlet of wine they were unable to bring to camp, along with the empty barrels they'd brought back. Titus tied a wine skin he'd refilled with water to the horn of the saddle.

The rest of the men had their assignments, and at this point, Titus could only hope they were in position. He had a short sword sheathed off his hip and his dagger tucked in his hem, but he'd not fought a full battle since he'd been injured. He knew he wouldn't be as fast, especially on his feet, and he prayed that when the fighting started, the surge of energy would carry him through.

Clip clop. Clip clop.

The horse plodded along slow and steady. The first part of his plan was to raise as little suspicion as possible.

Clip clop. Clip clop.

Titus guided the wagon around a turn and the palisade of the besieging army came into view, along with two guards at the gate and four surrounding the perimeter. Each stood near a long torch staked into the ground. The smokey aroma of roasting meat wafted in the air. The men inside the palisade were likely sitting down for a pleasant dinner, unaware that it might be their last.

The guard at the gate held up a hand for Titus to stop, which he did. "Supplies," Titus said.

"We already got a resupply earlier today."

Titus shrugged. "More were sent. Got some wine." He tapped the rundlet behind him.

The guards smiled at the sight.

Titus lifted the wine skin off his saddle—the good stuff—and offered a wink. He tossed it to the guard nearest him, who dropped his sword to catch it.

"Now." Titus said.

Horace sprang up from the wagon and took aim with his bow at the remaining armed guard. An arrow sailed through the air and tagged him in the chest before he could raise his weapon.

Titus spurred the horse forward before the other guard could retrieve his sword. The animal trampled over the man and Titus maneuvered the wagon in front of the gate to block it from opening.

The other guards shouted. "Attack! Attack!"

Titus unsheathed his short sword and swung down, slashing the hitching reins between the horse and carriage. They couldn't have the animal getting spooked and removing their blockade.

Horace took aim at another guard and dropped him. Titus's infantry men stormed out of the trees and cut down the remaining guards. The units around the castle took notice and mobilized, but arrows zipped out from the shadows, causing them to scramble for cover.

Soldiers within the palisade tried to open the gate, but the wagon kept it from budging more than a few inches. Titus grabbed a torch and lit the wagon on fire to prevent too many men from pushing on the door. Within seconds, it was ablaze.

An enemy soldier scaled the wall, but Horace targeted the man and dropped him.

The battle had begun flawlessly, but Titus's men fought on borrowed time. More enemy soldiers would scale the walls, and the units around the perimeter would eventually realize there was only one lone archer in the shadows for each group. Titus didn't have the numbers to do more. He had presented like he had a larger force to buy time and keep them pinned down, but the ruse didn't last long. The first unit figured it out and charged toward the palisade with swords raised.

Victory was now out of their hands. The men in the castle had to respond, or they'd have no chance. Titus had hoped the burning wagon would serve as a signal for them to rally, but so far, no one came.

As the enemy guards raced across the clearing, Titus gripped his sword, ready to fight until the end. He would not go down easily, and he had one more surprise in his arsenal. The five knights, led by Knut, charged in on horseback and engaged the guard unit. Knut kept the line tight, and they careened into the enemy, cutting them down in seconds.

It might've been a turning point in the battle with Titus's men gaining the upper hand, but the burning wagon began to crumble from the hungry flames. The soldiers in the palisade seized the opportunity and pushed against the gate with more force. It was about to give. Once the gate opened, a swarm of enemy troops would storm out and overwhelm them. If Titus didn't call a retreat, they'd all be annihilated.

He opened his mouth to shout the order when battle cries echoed in the distance. The castle gate opened and at least three dozen knights raced out on horseback and another three dozen infantry and archers dashed behind with swords and bows.

The guard units outside the clearing engaged, but many had already suffered a casualty from Titus's archers. They weren't prepared to be outnumbered. A dozen of the castle knights sped toward the palisade. Any enemy soldier that cleared the wall was immediately cut down.

When archers from the castle reached the enemy encampment, Horace organized them in a line facing the gate. As the doors cracked open and soldiers streamed out, they were met with a hail of arrows. Bodies dropped, creating more obstacles for the men behind. Knut positioned his knights nearby, cutting and cleaving anyone who escaped the barrage of missiles. When they were joined by the castle knights, the remaining enemy realized their doomed fate if they continued to fight. The survivors dashed away, either down the trail or into the trees.

Titus and his men had won. Fennelworth had been liberated!

Knut and the other men hugged their brethren from the castle. It was a joyous reunion and the night only got better as they looted Marmaduke's camp. Rundlets of wine, barrels of mead, and jugs of ale were all carted back to the castle. The men also took the meat they smelled cooking before the battle for a giant feast.

Titus remained and counted the dead. Two hundred of the besiegers had been killed. Miraculously, they'd only lost two men. Such a low casualty rate was almost unheard of, but it was not zero. Titus knelt beside the bodies, closed their eyes, and offered a quiet prayer for their souls.

The battle may have been won, but the war was far from over. More people would die.

CHAPTER 25

Men sang victory songs and drowned their trauma with ale in the castle's bailey. Titus searched for someone in charge and recognized two lower nobles. He made eye contact with the larger of the two, Rodrik. "How many soldiers do we have?"

Rodrik stopped his frivolity and approached Titus. "We have two hundred and three men at arms."

The words struck Titus hard. "It can't be. Marmaduke killed almost two thousand at Kent?"

"We don't know how many were killed," Rodrik said. "Some fled into the forest. They've likely deserted."

Titus didn't know how to react to the news and stood dumbfounded. In a best case, Marmaduke's army only numbered one thousand, but that assumed he'd not added any recruits or mercenaries. The combined total of their forces was two hundred and thirty-two men. After everything they'd gone through to liberate Fennelworth, they still had no chance against Marmaduke.

Titus comforted himself with the thought of food. At least they wouldn't have to worry about that for a while. "Show me what we have to work with." He waved his hand toward the castle, in part to change the subject.

Rodrik swallowed and led Titus and Knut inside to give a tour of their provisions. When they reached the cellar beneath the kitchen, mostly empty shelves greeted them.

"Is this it?" Titus asked.

Rodrik nodded.

Titus opened a bag of wheat. Half full. Beside it, two burlap sacks of turnips, and next to that, a haunch of venison that already showed signs of spoiling. Titus searched the room, hoping Rodrik had been mistaken. If they hadn't come when they did, the castle would have been forced to surrender in a week.

"Let me show you the armory," Rodrik said, eager to leave. He waved them back up the steps.

Titus stopped in the kitchen and leaned forward against the table. What was the point of visiting the armory? They didn't have the men to wield anymore weapons.

"Is there something else I can show you?" Rodrik asked.

Titus didn't respond and kept his emotions simmering inside.

Rodrik rubbed his palms together.

Knut held up a hand for Rodrik to relax. "It's okay."

"The castle had not been prepped for a siege," Rodrik explained, perhaps afraid of being blamed for the dire situation.

Titus ignored the comment and weighed their options. If Marmaduke returned with a larger sieging force, they'd be the ones in need of rescue, but the freezing cold of Black Mountain wasn't a viable alternative either. There were too many people to keep hidden, and he needed to feed them. Titus's head began to throb more than his shoulder.

"Where's Lord Kensington?" Rodrik asked.

"He went north to find more troops," Knut said.

Titus didn't share his own feelings about the king's whereabouts. Like the missing soldiers, he feared Kensington may have deserted, too.

The silence lingered for too long until Knut asked the obvious, "Should I order the men to gather what we can and leave?"

The high of the victory followed by the low of the aftermath left Titus paralyzed with indecision. Physically he was on empty, too. The battle exhausted his body and did nothing to help his aching injuries. Fortunately, the threat of a Marmaduke attack wasn't imminent. It would take at least a day for him to mobilize.

"I will address the soldiers in the morning." Titus left the kitchen.

He ambled down the hallway and passed a handful of half-drunk soldiers. They shouted as a show of support for their leader. The sound didn't register, and neither did the men singing and dancing in the bailey, but the frigid air did. It carried a bite he'd not noticed before. Titus grabbed a torch hanging on the wall and slipped into the darkened chapel. He wanted to be alone. Fortunately, people only entered the sacred place to pray, and they were preoccupied with ale. The flame illuminated the space with a warm glow as Titus hung the torch on a sconce. He paused at the sight of the wooden cross mounted in front of a large stained glass window. The symbol used to mean so much, but that ended when his wife died. The rest of the small room was unremarkable, with four stone pews, two on each side. Titus curled up on the one farthest from the cross and turned his back to it.

His exhaustion was so complete that he should've fallen asleep immediately, but he couldn't. The singing from the bailey could no longer be ignored. The joyous lyrics gnawed at him. *Could the men not see they celebrated their funerals?*

A depressing anger simmered, which furthered his restlessness. How had he ended up leading a doomed army? After Kensington left, it just sort of happened. He carried no title or official mandate from the absentee king. If anything, Knut should carry the burden. He'd been made a duke and wanted desperately for people to look up to him.

Titus wanted to leave. To desert. If the king could do it, why couldn't he? The blood of these men would not be on him. He would welcome the shame of fleeing over the guilt of leading everyone to their deaths. If he snuck away in the black of night, no one would even notice. He'd say he needed to search the enemy camp and then never come back. When morning arrived, the men would figure it out and either rally around Knut or they'd desert like the others. Titus hoped for the latter. The war would be over, but they'd be alive.

A muffled rustling caused Titus to freeze. He wasn't alone, but the noise sounded distant and came from the ground. Was someone trying to burrow into the castle?

Titus got to his feet, removed the torch from the wall, and shuffled to the staircase leading into the kings' crypt. With the torch in one hand, he pulled the dagger from his hem with the other. As he descended, the temperature dropped. When he reached the bottom, the light from the flame revealed six stone sarcophagi. Three had the image of a bearded man, but different men. All held a sword in front of their chest with both hands and the blade running down to their knees. These were the past kings. Beside each was their queen, or in some cases, their favorite queen. The sarcophagus of King Charles was furthest away.

For the briefest of moments, Titus forgot about the noise that had drawn him into the tomb, and he stared at the carved image of his friend. Guilt tugged at his conscience for never having paid his last respects. He stepped further into the crypt. Something moved to his left.

Titus turned and held the dagger in front. "Who goes there?"

A figure stood up. It was Michael.

"Michael?" Titus lowered the blade. "What are you doing down here?"

"I... I was sleeping," Michael stuttered.

"Why aren't you inside the castle?" Titus asked.

"I'm not one of the soldiers."

"You're also not a dead king."

Michael looked away, embarrassed. Titus didn't intend for his words to sound so harsh. "And you're more of a soldier than most of them, Michael. Few would've risked their lives sneaking up to the castle walls."

The boy nodded, but still kept his head low.

King Charles's sarcophagus drew Titus over. The etched image of the king captured his heavy chin and sharp cheekbones, but it was impossible to replicate the eyes in stone. They didn't portray the king's penetrating stare or that magical sparkle that caused men to do anything that fell from his lips.

"I met him," Michael said.

Titus raised an eyebrow, intrigued. "*You* met the king?"

"Sort of. King Charles came to our village twice," Michael said. "The first time was many years ago, when I was little. He came after the wheat harvest and asked if he could join us for Lammas. He told us he loved the holiday and the bread we made was his favorite."

Titus bit his tongue, unwilling to taint the memory. Charles often complimented people right before asking something from them. He likely increased the wheat tax after the visit and the people gladly payed. "And the second time?" Titus asked.

"He came after the plague ended." Michael furrowed his brow as he recalled the visit. "He was different. Frail. His beard had turned white. He apologized he could not stop the plague, and he said he'd do whatever he could to support his people."

Titus struggled to imagine his friend as an old man with a white beard. Charles had always been full of vigor and optimism.

"And he did," Michael said. "He lowered our taxes and gave us oxen to help plow our fields. He was a great man. I will fight to the death for him."

The words paused Titus and brought him back to reality. "Michael, there may come a point when you need to run. Just like you did when Marmaduke came."

Michael shook his head. "I don't want to run anymore. Marmaduke is going to pay—"

Titus sliced the air with his hand to cut him off. "Promise me that when that time comes, you will run."

"But what if I can help? Like with the arrow. What if that's the difference between us winning?"

"Your parents would want you to live, Michael. There will come a point where there's nothing left to do. Promise me that when that happens, you will leave."

Michael's brow furrowed. "You say that as if you know we're going to lose."

Titus didn't respond, but his silence spoke for him.

"We just broke the siege. How can you believe we have no chance?"

"We don't have the numbers. I thought we'd have more men here. We don't even have enough food. At some point, we'll either starve or we'll face Marmaduke's full army. We can't win against that. You *need* to leave."

"Why should I leave if you're going to stay and fight?"

"I never said I was going to stay."

The words caused Michael to recoil. "*You're* leaving?"

"We can't stay, Michael. If Marmaduke comes with his army, we will all die."

Michael shook his head in disgust. "You're not the real Titus."

Titus refused to let the insult impact his decision. "I don't know who that is, Michael. I'm just trying to save your life."

Michael glared at Titus and then sat back down defiantly.

Titus pursed his lips and swatted his hand in Michael's direction. "Get yourself killed then." He climbed the steps and left the chapel in a huff. The soldiers still celebrated in the bailey, but he marched past them until he reached the main gate. He motioned for the guard to open it. "I need to search the encampment for supplies."

The guard nodded and pulled the heavy beam back and then cracked the door. Titus slipped out and hurried down the trail, determined to get as far away as quickly as possible, but he couldn't outrun his conscience, which tortured him with horrible thoughts. He imagined Marmaduke gutting Michael and executing men like Knut and Horace. Titus shook off the guilt. It's why he had to leave. The soldiers might desert if he left. It was the right thing to do—the humane thing. When Titus pushed all the awful thoughts out of his mind, he exhaled with relief. But then, his son's last word echoed in his ears.

Why?

The sound was so distinct he looked around for its source, but he was alone. He still had no answer to his son's question, but there were other "whys". If God wanted Titus dead, why had he met Rosalind? Why had she healed his injuries? Why had he met Michael? Why couldn't Michael see he would die if he stayed?

Nothing made sense. Titus collapsed on his knees in despair. "What do you want from me, God?"

The forest remained silent, except for the buzzing of cicadas.

"I can't win this war. I can't do it."

A tear rolled down Titus's cheek. He might've stayed on the ground, broken forever, but something brushed against his nose. It left a slight tingle and chill. Then he felt it on his arm. Titus stared out across the night sky. Snowflakes floated down.

Winter had arrived.

Titus looked up at the heavens and shook his head in frustration. He knew what this meant. They could stay at the castle. At least for a while.

Titus pulled himself to his feet and turned back toward the castle.

CHAPTER 26

Under normal conditions, and if Kensington hadn't lost at Kent, they would've had at least a month to stock the castle with oats, barley, and salted meat. Marmaduke knew this. It's why he launched the siege. He displaced the villagers in the land surrounding the stronghold and raided their farms, leaving no crops. Limited prospects for hunting and foraging, coupled with the first snow of the season, meant that food options would be even scarcer.

The snow wasn't all bad, however. It brought one very important advantage, which gave Titus a sliver of hope, and it was the reason he stayed. Marmaduke wouldn't dare send a second force north, as no army had ever begun a siege in the snow. It wasn't practical to march soldiers through the cold and attempt to build a camp to protect them from the weather. It was more likely many would die from exposure or sickness. Without the threat of another siege, Titus's small army could remain at Fennelworth with a roof over their heads.

Despite the low risk of attack, Titus refused to take any chances and gathered the troops in the bailey. "Men, we need to hurry. I need three men to monitor Marmaduke's forces and make sure they're not mobilizing."

Four individuals and Michael raised their hands to volunteer. Titus ignored Michael and pointed to the first three.

"I also need forty men to go two miles south and cut ten large trees, so they block any army of size from advancing. Lastly, we must salvage any valuable items from the remnants of Marmaduke's camp. Wood. Clothing. Blankets. Anything."

Michael volunteered to chop the timbers along the main trail, but Titus ignored that, too. The young teen was left to scavenge, an assignment he groused about under his breath. Titus didn't react, and instead departed to help the men block the path.

If Marmaduke attempted a winter march, the logs would halt any wagons and carriages. The timbers weren't a permanent obstacle, but they would provide a few precious minutes for the castle to evacuate if necessary, and Titus planned to rotate one scout to monitor the trail at all times.

By day's end, the soldiers blocked the route, and Marmaduke's army showed no signs of mobilizing. With the defensive measures in place, the group retreated to the dining hall for a well-earned, albeit modest, meal. Titus sat with the troops, which resulted in stunted and awkward conversations. Meals were an opportunity for men to bond, commiserate, and share jokes, away from their superiors. No one wanted to state the obvious in front of Titus. Winter would be three months of harsh wind, ice, and snow. How would they survive?

When Titus finished his last bite, he stood and made eye contact with Horace and Knut. He didn't need to speak. His gaze said enough. The two offered a subtle nod and followed Titus through the dining hall and upstairs to the king's salon. Once they all were inside, Titus closed the door behind them.

"The supplies we scavenged from the besieging camp will give us another four or five days of food," he said.

"That's it?" Knut asked.

Titus nodded. The daunting challenge didn't need to be explained. They had over two hundred mouths to feed for all of winter. All three remained silent as they tried to think of a solution.

Knut rubbed his forehead. "If it comes to it, we can eat the horses." He tilted his chin in the direction of the stable. "Like that mangy one you came in on."

Titus shook his head. "That horse must be returned." Despite Titus's order, if the men didn't receive enough food, they'd take matters into their own hands, but if they ate the horses, the war would be over before another battle took place. Cavalry was essential for warfare. On top of that, if they needed to evacuate, the animals would be critical for hauling supplies.

Knut shrugged and let out a sputtering sigh. "Then we must feed them, too."

"We also need firewood," Horace said. "It's only going to get colder."

"And more space," Knut added. "Eventually, someone will fall ill and we'll need to isolate them or we'll all have it."

The problems multiplied, which left Titus pacing the room while stroking his chin. "Take a census of the men. Find the best hunters, fishermen, and trappers. We must have units to gather firewood, twigs, and grasses for the horses, and we will build more shelter in the bailey. Nobility does not matter. The best shall lead these tasks."

Knut refused to acknowledge the statement, but he also didn't challenge it. He and Horace turned to leave, but Titus held up his hand. "Wait." The men paused.

"Assign Michael to gather firewood."

"What if he's good at hunting?" Horace asked.

"Firewood," Titus said.

Horace nodded despite the conflicting statements. He and Knut left to execute the orders, leaving Titus to his thoughts. Perhaps Kensington would return with help. If he learned of the castle's liberation, it was possible. But it was more likely Kensington would never return.

THE TEMPERATURE DROPPED, and the snow continued. Titus squeezed everyone inside the castle, an unusual move. A typical army would've camped in the courtyard under makeshift tents while the high-ranking nobles slept inside. Titus never accepted such elitism, so he ordered the armory cleared, and he moved the furniture from the king's salon into the bailey. Every man would be warm and dry.

The new quartering arrangement gave Horace and Knut the opportunity to ask the men questions about their talents. Several of the nobles rattled off their family's resumes. Others praised their dueling abilities as if that would make them an expert hunter. A few possessed actual hunting experience, but it was limited to wild boar for sport, and there weren't any near Fennelworth. Ultimately, most of the gentry weren't skilled at much beyond battle and being noble.

Out of all the aristocrats, only one had a useful survival skill. Walter knew how to fish. He had grown up by a lake where his family obtained a majority of their sustenance. As the most seasoned fisherman, Knut placed him in command of ten infantrymen with less experience. The rest of the nobility were assigned to collect food for the horses and gather firewood. Many egos were bruised as a result.

Trapping fell to three common foot soldiers who had spent years capturing small game. They were put in charge of ten men with slightly less knowledge. Their orders were clear—train the others to build and set as many snares as possible. They could even use the castle's blacksmith to make more elaborate and robust traps for larger game.

A second group of infantrymen had expertise in foraging. Their goal was to gather nuts, herbs, mushrooms, and roughage. There wouldn't be much this late in the year, but any nutrients would help. They'd deliver everything to the castle's cooks for storage and rationing.

The archers, unsurprisingly, had the most relevant hunting experience. They were organized into small groups to hunt deer, pheasant, and rabbit.

Everyone else, including the castle's priest, was tasked with finding building materials for more lodgings and to gather food for the horses. Titus watched from a distance as the last soldier received their assignment. From the corner, Michael walked over to Horace. "I'd like to forage," he said.

"Uh, we have enough for that, young lad. We need help with firewood."

"I'm better at foraging. I did it for years for my family."

Horace glanced over at Titus, then back at Michael. "Maybe another time."

The men settled in for a rough night of sleep. If the howling winds didn't keep a man awake, then the snoring of a few did. Still, it was better than sleeping in the cold.

At dawn, the soldiers exited the castle's cozy interior and gathered in the courtyard where a blanket of white greeted them. The dusting of snow would make daily life harder, but it wouldn't stop the men from carrying out their duties. They had no choice. Last night had been a mild storm, and winter had only just begun.

OVER THE NEXT SEVERAL DAYS, everyone worked grueling hours. Not a single individual rested, as all knew the dire stakes if they failed their assignments. Each man toiled to his physical limit, trying to squeeze two months of work into a week, and the results, though impressive, fell well short to carry them through winter. Walter's fishing expedition yielded thirty fish of various sizes. The archers felled one deer, five rabbits, and four pheasants. The foragers collected handfuls of nuts, mushrooms, nettles, and wild carrots. In addition, they had built a simple wooden lodge in the bailey's corner. The meager dwelling could sleep twenty and would be used for anyone who got sick. Lastly, the men stockpiled cords of firewood against the inside of the castle walls, along with twigs, bark, and grass for the horses.

The efforts would've continued, but on the eighth day, ominous black clouds rolled over the hills. The winds picked up, and a brought a biting chill. The first major storm of the season was upon them.

Within minutes, a sprinkle of snow turned into icy blasts and the wind shrieked as if to announce the tempest's arrival. Horace and Knut rode through the forest, shouting at anyone they came across. "Get in the castle! Now!"

The men scampered through the flurries to the safety of the walls. Horace guided the final group of archers to the castle and Knut ushered the last of the foragers back as chunks of ice pelted them. When they entered the gate, the doors slammed and the large beam slid into place. Everyone hurried inside the dining hall and surrounding rooms to get warm and ride out the storm.

Noble and common soldier sat together and joked while ale was brought out from the cellar. Titus went from table to table in the dining hall and chatted with various individuals. Having worked closely with the men over the recent days, he'd learned many of their names. There was Garrett from Devonsbrook, but men called him "Red" because of his unusual hair color. Nimby Nobs took no issue from the jokes people made about his name. Most of those jokes were told by Peter Longwood, the resident jester. Titus overheard one of Peter's yarns and couldn't help but laugh, which caught everyone off guard.

"Oh, Lord." Peter lifted his head toward the heavens. "I'll never doubt you again. You may have parted the seas for Moses, but no one thought it possible to bring a smile to this man's face." Peter motioned to Titus, which brought more laughter.

Titus's smile turned into a scowl and a hush fell upon the hall. The awkward silence caused Peter to swallow. Titus held the moment and then grinned. He was only playing. Titus patted Peter on the back, causing the men to guffaw. He'd pulled one over on the group, including the jokester. Titus continued greeting people and was surprised, relieved even, that everyone had responded so well to the challenging circumstances. Maybe they had hope after all. His respite was short-lived as something dawned on him. Michael wasn't there.

CHAPTER 27

Titus pulled Horace aside. "Where's Michael?"

Horace shook his head and then turned to the soldier in charge of firewood. "Where's the boy?"

The soldier shrugged.

Titus rushed out of the dining hall, across the bailey, and into the chapel. "Michael?" he shouted.

No answer.

Titus returned to the castle and hurried through the remaining rooms, hoping to find Michael hiding in a corner. As he passed each group of men, he asked, "Have you seen the boy?"

Heads shook.

A hard gust of wind cracked against the wooden shutters, which only intensified Titus's worry.

A soldier walked up behind Titus. "I think I saw him."

Titus whirled around. "Where and when?"

"He was foraging near the river. A couple of hours ago."

Titus raced back outside and across the courtyard, and then into the stable. He saddled the fittest horse in minutes and led it to the main gate.

"Open it," he barked.

The guard slid the beam out and cracked the door. A gust of wind whooshed inside. Titus mounted the horse and kicked his heels into its sides. The animal snorted and charged away, galloping over the fresh snow. In seconds, the castle shrank and disappeared in the distance. Titus guided the stallion off the trail and the unsteady terrain forced him to slow down. The snow had covered rocks, holes, and sticks, so the horse needed to find its footing with every step.

When Titus reached the river's edge, he called out, "Michael?"

A faint trickle of river water answered. The edges had already frozen, and in a few more hours the whole thing would be a sheet of ice.

Titus kept following the stream while calling out. "Michael?"

Still nothing.

The idea of Michael being gone forever itched in Titus's stomach. The wind blasted through the trees, and the biting cold cut through his coat. A lump formed in Titus's throat. No one could survive out here. Not for long, anyway. The stallion neighed as if to beckon Titus back to the castle. The animal instinctively knew the danger they were in. With shaky hands, Titus pulled the reins around, but as the horse turned, movement caught his eye.

Titus whirled back and squinted. *Was that an arm waving in the distance?* Titus spurred the steed, and in minutes, Titus found Michael lying on the ground, shivering. He dismounted and rushed over.

Teeth chattering, the teen muttered, "I ffffeelll in the waaaater."

"It's okay, Michael." Titus pulled him up. Both man and boy groaned. Titus's arm and leg ached from the extra weight, but he allowed Michael's entire body to lean against him as the two hobbled to the steed. "Get your foot in the stirrup."

Michael tried to follow the order, but it took three tries.

"I need you to hoist yourself. I'll push from behind."

Michael nodded, and Titus pushed with all his strength. The boy heaved himself up and then lay face down on the rump of the horse. Titus mounted the animal and then kicked his heels into its side.

"Hang on, Michael." Titus held onto the boy with one hand while holding the reins with the other.

The storm increased in intensity, as if intentionally fighting them, and the whiteout conditions made it impossible for Titus to see more than a few feet. He rode close enough to the river while praying for a break in the weather so he could find a landmark that would let him know he was near the castle.

After several minutes, the horse lurched to its right. Titus hoped that the animal had some memory or could smell how to get back. The stallion stepped through the trees and the area opened up. They'd found the main trail.

As soon as they reached the castle, Titus ordered men to carry Michael to the king's bedroom, where they got him out of the wet clothes and covered with blankets. His face had a tint of blue and his eyes slid open and shut. Titus leaned Michael up and tilted a cup of hot water to his lips, trying to force him to drink, but it dribbled out of his mouth and he slipped unconscious. Nothing else could be done. Either the boy's body would warm itself or he'd die.

Titus pulled a small wooden chair by the bed and sat. When Ariella and Aidan were sick or dying, Titus had prayed, something he refused to do now since it hadn't done any good. He leaned forward toward Michael, eyes bearing down as if he could will the boy's recovery.

One by one, the other men left, leaving Titus and the boy alone. There was no sound except for Michael's shallow breaths.

Hours passed and Michael didn't stir. Titus ignored the fact that Michael might not make it, but as minutes slipped by, the possibility gnawed at him. *Was life just sorrow and suffering?* Titus couldn't handle another loss. If Michael died, he didn't have the strength to continue leading the men. More time ticked away, and Titus remained by his side, almost in a catatonic state.

A giant burst of wind slammed against the shutters. The boy rolled over and his eyes cracked. Titus opened his mouth to speak, but the relief and fatigue hit him all at once and his head drooped.

"I'm sorry," Michael said in a raspy and weak voice.

"What were you thinking?" Titus asked.

"I wanted to help," Michael said. "I wanted to be like the other men. Like a soldier."

Titus shook his head. The boy didn't get it. "Soldiers kill or soldiers die, Michael."

Michael swallowed and lifted his chin. "Soldiers fight. I am going to fight Marmaduke. For my family—" his voice cracked.

Titus's head drooped again. The boy's stubbornness would get him killed. He took a deep breath. "I had a son. Did you know that?"

Michael shook his head.

"Marmaduke killed him." Titus's jaw clenched, the words still difficult for him to say.

Michael's furrowed brow softened.

"You need to live, Michael. *I* will fight." Titus tapped a

finger against his chest. "It's what I was made for, but you…" He gestured at the boy. "You must live."

"Why? Why me?"

Titus leaned back and fumbled for an explanation. "Someone must live." He shook his head, unable to come up with a better answer, and then pointed at Michael. "But I will only fight if you promise me you won't do anything stupid like this again." Titus's uncomfortable gaze bore down on the boy.

Michael's jaw clenched and his eyes welled up. The burning anger and hate blinded him, but he had no chance on the battlefield. If revenge was his aim, then Titus was his best option. He stared back at the grizzled man in front of him. "Are you *the* Titus?"

The old warrior had spent years trying to bury the memories of the prior war. He'd never felt like the figure people spoke of, and he tried to pretend someone else had done the horrific things he'd done. His eyes dropped to the floor. "I am the Titus who fought in the war against the three wicked barons."

Neither needed to say anything further. They'd struck a deal.

CHAPTER 28

Within two days, Michael had recovered from his plunge into the icy river. When he felt well enough to leave the king's bedroom, he kept his end of the bargain and only did safe chores around the castle, which brought the weight of Titus's promise to bear. Each time Titus made eye contact with Michael, knots filled his stomach. He needed to be both King Charles and the legendary warrior, and he was neither.

Fighting had always been the thing he was best at, but his body still hadn't fully healed from the battle of Kent. Sure, he could wield a sword, but he was no match for a skilled knight. To regain his form, Titus had to utilize every available minute, even though winter made traditional training impossible.

While the storm battered the castle, he stretched his body, but the scar tissue in the shoulder joint stopped him from lifting his arm above his head, and the thigh injury prevented him from squatting without leaning to the uninjured side. Each time he extended a limb, he pushed himself until the pain became unbearable.

Once the weather improved, he trotted around the castle walls to increase his leg strength and endurance. After that, he shadow dueled alone to improve his mobility. As he practiced, Titus imagined Enok, Marmaduke's gargantuan henchman. The beast of a man was unlike anyone Titus had ever faced, even during the war against the barons. He'd never be able to match the giant's muscles. Agility and speed were his only hope.

Titus moved from side to side, deflecting imaginary strikes, while countering with slashes and stabs from his short sword. Despite the progress, Titus's movements weren't fluid or instinctive. He hoped the reason was because he practiced against a pretend foe. The only way to find out for sure was a duel with an opponent, and there was only one available soldier who could've challenged Titus in his prime—Knut.

Titus found the big man sitting in the dining hall with the other soldiers. "Knut, may I have a word with you?"

Knut obliged the request and followed Titus upstairs. "Where are we going?" he asked.

Titus guided Knut into the king's chamber and shut the door. "I'd like to duel."

"Why not do it in the bailey?" Knut asked.

"I think it would be best if we did it here."

"Afraid I'm going to beat you?" Knut smirked, but it faded when Titus didn't respond. "Alright. Let's have at it." Knut unsheathed his sword as did Titus.

Both men straddled their feet and circled one another in defensive stances. Titus attacked first, swinging his blade to the right, then to the left. Knut stepped back and Titus attempted to capitalize on the retreat, but he leaned too far, lost his footing, and tumbled to the floor. Knut didn't have to do anything further. If it were actual combat, Titus would've been killed.

"Again." Titus stood and lifted his sword, ready for another round.

Knut nodded, and the two clashed swords. After multiple strikes and parries, Titus swung too hard and his momentum left him exposed for a belly strike. Knut's blade touched his midsection. Neither man needed to confirm the outcome.

"Again," Titus said through heavy breath.

The duel resumed and after swings, deflections, and clanging of metal, Knut's sword tip ended up pointed at Titus's gut. Try as he might, and he did a dozen more times, Titus could not compete against Knut. His strikes and steps were too slow. Finally, he declared, "Enough."

Knut could've mocked Titus's performance, but he didn't. He bowed and made for the door.

"Wait," Titus said.

Knut stopped and turned.

Titus had barely given Knut a workout and though he wanted to take the high road, losing for the first time bothered him. "When you attack to the left," Titus said in a conciliatory tone, "you signal it with your shoulder. A faster opponent will take advantage." It was the best Titus could muster.

Knut nodded and walked down the steps to the dining hall. The big man's silence worsened the defeat. Warriors of comparable skill took pleasure in ribbing one another after a dueling victory, but there was no joy in defeating someone incapable of winning.

Titus had lost his edge, and he didn't know how to get it back.

THE WINTER DAYS PLODDED ALONG. The tortuous cold, tedious chores and constant hunger made each week feel like a month, but winter also meant they were safe. Whenever the weather warmed, even for an afternoon, an edginess filled the walls. Was spring coming early? Would Marmaduke attack?

Titus continued to dispatch spies south to collect information, and the updates were mixed. Early in the season, they'd learned Marmaduke had permitted the infantrymen who were farmers to return home and harvest their crops on the condition they contribute a large share to the mercenaries who stayed with him at Doldren Castle. Unfortunately, he didn't sit idle while he filled his belly. He also sent emissaries further east to gather more funding and support.

So, while Marmaduke's troops remained well fed and grew in strength, Titus's army struggled to survive, and by the second half of the season, they found themselves on borrowed time. The hunters didn't even see deer or pheasants anymore. The lake had been over-fished, and the small game they trapped yielded bites for each man, not meals. Unless something changed, they would not make it to spring.

As the reality set in, morale plummeted. Meals, which had once been a time for playful banter and bonding, turned into grousing and grumbling sessions. Peter, the unofficial court jester, no longer told jokes, but no one was in the mood to laugh, anyway. Things only got worse when Titus informed them they'd need to get by with one meal a day.

During the first dinner of increased rationing, Titus sat at the end of the dining hall and ate his paltry portion, that comprised a small venison chunk, half a carrot, and a few bites of bread. As he chewed, a soldier smacked his fist against the table. "Why do we starve when we have lots of meat in the stables?"

Silence descended upon the room and eyes shifted to Titus. The animals had been on everyone's mind, but no one had said anything until now. It was a moment Titus had feared. He wanted to believe that Kensington would return with reinforcements and supplies, but there'd been no news from him since he'd left.

"I know we are all hungry," Titus began.

As he spoke, a scout rushed into the hall with scared eyes. Titus didn't want him to reveal more bad news in front of the group. They had enough to contend with already. Titus motioned for him to go into the king's salon. "We will discuss this when I return." He led the scout upstairs, with Knut and Horace following.

As soon as the door shut, the scout delivered the latest. "Marmaduke has reached a deal with the Earl of Graymark."

"Graymark?" Knut asked with surprise.

Graymark was a powerful noble from a faraway territory in the east. He'd remained neutral in conflicts that didn't impact his land. Instead of fighting, he'd used the time to build trading alliances and become filthy rich.

"What did Marmaduke promise him?" Titus asked.

"I don't know, but Marmaduke's getting two thousand in gold."

"Bloody hell," Horace said.

That amount of money would allow Marmaduke to buy a lot more troops, food, and equipment. Titus assumed Marmaduke promised large territories in the north that were yet to be conquered. There was no other explanation.

"When will he receive the money?" Titus asked.

The scout hesitated to deliver the worst of the news. "It's already on its way."

An emptiness filled the room. Come spring, and maybe sooner, Marmaduke would have everything he needed for a major and sustained assault.

The door flew open and Michael entered. "The men are fighting!"

Titus charged down the stairs, with everyone following. A handful of soldiers traded blows in the center of the hall, while the rest shouted in a ring around them.

Titus jumped in the fray and pulled men off each other. "Enough," he screamed. Knut also yanked the combatants apart.

Several continued throwing punches and kicks. A couple had bloody noses and bruises across their faces. Within seconds, Titus and Knut had stopped the fight, but angry shouts persisted.

"The cowards are talking about leaving," one of the bleeding knights said.

"We have to. We'll die if we stay here," Nimby Nobs said.

"Enough," Titus shouted again.

The room quieted down.

A bruised soldier wiped blood off his face. "What are we doing about food?"

"We have at least another month of winter. We must eat the horses," Nimby said.

Titus sliced the air with his hand. "No."

"Then we must take from the villages?"

"No," Titus said. "Marmaduke steals from people. We will not be like him."

"Then we will die," Nimby said.

Titus shook his head. "No, we will steal from Marmaduke."

The men side-eyed each other. Titus could not be suggesting a winter attack. No one could remember the last winter battle. It's the reason they'd been safe in their castle. And had he forgotten the size of Marmaduke's army?

"The Earl of Graymark is sending a caravan to Marmaduke with two thousand in gold. I say that money should go to support *our* army." Titus pointed to the group.

The men stared at Titus with bewildered expressions.

Titus gestured outside. "It's still winter. The caravan will not expect an attack, especially from us."

"But we need food. We don't need gold," a soldier called out.

"We can buy food, and the caravan will still have supplies for the men traveling," Titus said.

No one responded. Their silence revealed their skepticism.

"Graymark is a long way away," Titus said. "The soldiers will also be tired."

One of the bloodied soldiers stepped forward. "Marmaduke has men watching us, the same way we're watching him."

This fact did present a problem. If they mobilized everyone, or a large group of soldiers, Marmaduke would find out. He might intercept Titus's troops, ending the war, or overpower the castle if Titus left it poorly defended.

"We leave tonight. Twenty of us. We double up on horses. No one will suspect us leaving then, and it's a small enough force to remain hidden or dismissed as a foraging run."

"But is it large enough to take out the knights guarding the caravan?" a soldier asked.

Titus could only hope that it was.

CHAPTER 29

Twenty men departed Fennelworth at midnight, two on each horse. Titus brought ten archers and ten knights, including himself. Horace and Knut were among them. The group carried heavy rope and several axes. Based on reports from Titus's informants, the earl's caravan would be coming that day, so they had no time to spare. They followed the northern trail first and then cut east through the forest before turning south in case any spies watched the path. They rode through the trees until they'd passed the blockade of logs. After that, they rode along the trail as fast as they could, hoping to get well east of Marmaduke's castle before morning.

As dawn broke, the snowdrifts on the ground thinned, but the tree branches and bushes still had a white dusting. Titus eyed the timbers carefully while they rode by. The location Titus chose needed to be perfect for the series of traps and diversions he envisioned, and it had to include a mix of evergreen and deciduous trees. The evergreens provided plenty of hiding spots and the deciduous trees had heavier branches. Titus held up his hand when he spotted tree limbs stretching over the trail in multiple places. The small band of warriors stopped and got to work.

All but one archer scouted the area for hiding places with good shooting angles. The remaining bowman traveled east along the path to stand watch.

Three of the knights led the horses into the forest and tied their reins behind a thick cluster of trees. Meanwhile, Knut hacked away at the base of a large pine forty yards west of the ambush site. The rest of the knights found two large dead trees and carried them to the sides of the trail. They used the axes to chop each tree into two pieces. They threw ends of the ropes over branches hanging high across the path and then secured them to the logs. The heavy slabs of wood required all hands to hoist them into the air and then tie them to the nearest trunk. Before they lifted the fourth log, the lookout galloped back.

"They're coming," the breathless man sputtered.

Everyone scrambled into position. Most knights hid under snow covered bushes close to the road, and the archers took cover behind timbers further away. Three knights concealed themselves by the trees where the ropes holding the logs had been mounted. Each gripped an axe. Knut stayed down the trail beside the large pine that had almost been chopped down.

A deathly stillness filled the forest as the men laid in wait. The path remained empty, and after several minutes, men glanced at one another, wondering if their scout had been mistaken. But then, a knight on horseback trotted around the bend.

He was point for the caravan. His unenviable job was to search the area and flush out any ambushes before the contingent behind him arrived. Titus's men knew not to attack until the main force had reached them.

Seconds later, more horsemen emerged. Titus counted in his head as a stream of soldiers emerged. Ten mounted knights followed by ten crossbowmen on foot and then two coachmen whose horses pulled a covered carriage. Behind them, even more mounted knights, and more crossbowmen. Forty fighters total. The imposing caravan paused Titus. There were too many. He wanted to call off the attack, but he'd not given any instruction or signal *not* to attack. Horace was told to fire as soon as the last man passed him. That moment was now!

The arrow zipped out from the trees and tagged a crossbowman in the chest. His comrades beside him turned in shock, only to find more arrows targeting them. Several found their mark.

"Ambush. It's an ambush!" an enemy knight shouted.

The horsemen unsheathed their swords and maneuvered their horses around.

All eyes shifted toward Horace's side of the trail. One of Titus's men on the opposite side cut a rope, causing a log to swing down from the trees. It smashed into three knights on horseback, sending them careening to the ground.

The enemy crossbowman searched for targets, but only found walls of trees with arrows whizzing out. Many fired without aiming, hoping to hit something, which left them exposed as they reloaded, a much harder process in the cold. Enemy knights circled back and split up so they could defend both sides.

Titus's men cut two more ropes, one from each side. Logs swung down. The knights moved to avoid the log they saw, but unfortunately they stepped their horses into the path of the one they didn't. Eight were swept off their animals, and either killed or knocked unconscious.

More volleys of arrows zinged from the branches and disrupted the enemy forces further.

"Run," a crossbowman said.

A panic started and one coachman cracked the reins against

the horses pulling the carriage. The animals charged forward and barreled through three of their own men.

Knut chopped away at the tree as the carriage approached. It was going to be tight as the log creaked and teetered. Knut dropped the axe and pushed with all his might. The wood at the base cracked, and the tree tilted more until gravity gained the upper hand. *Whoosh!*

As the giant timber fell, the coachmen stared in horror. The horses passed the log a split second before it thundered down and smashed into the carriage. The coachmen's seats split from the rest of the wagon and the horses dragged them away down the path.

Titus's knights charged out from the bushes and struck down anyone who hadn't fled. Titus tried to join the fight, but his slow legs didn't help, and it was over by the time he reached the trail. The enemy either lay dead at his feet or they scattered in all directions.

Titus shook his head in disbelief while catching his breath. The victory had been so decisive, and it had all happened so fast. He began counting his men and searching the fallen. A few of his knights had minor injuries, but they'd not suffered a single casualty.

The soldiers were already crowded around the carriage. Time for the spoils. The front was smashed, but the back remained intact. The men busted the door and discovered barrels of bread and meat, along with six chests. They bashed the metal locks and lifted the lids. A spontaneous cheer erupted from the men. Half of the boxes contained a heaping of gold coins and the other half was silver.

"Good luck paying your mercenaries now," one soldier joked.

Men laughed and offered other insults, while Titus forced himself between two soldiers and got a look at the haul. It was far more than two thousand. It might've been triple that amount. The relief Titus had felt just a moment earlier vanished, replaced with a sickening dread. His fists clenched, and the heat from his breath billowed out in a small cloud with every rapid exhale. "Collect everything of value. We need to return to Fennelworth quickly."

The attack was an unmitigated success, with an unexpectedly large bounty, but that was the problem. That amount of money meant one thing. If Marmaduke didn't deliver on his end of the deal with Graymark, he was a dead man. They'd poked the sleeping bear, and now the bear had to respond.

CHAPTER 30

Titus and the soldiers rushed back to Fennelworth. As they rode into the bailey, the men in the castle received them like conquering heroes shouting cries of victory. Then, a chant started, "Titus! Titus! Titus!"

Titus ignored the celebration and dismounted. He held up his hands for quiet. "We must abandon the castle. Gather all the weapons and everything we need to survive."

The men stared at each other, dumbfounded. Titus disappeared into the stronghold and made his way to the king's salon. He sat down, but his fists clenched involuntarily. His heart raced and his chest heaved in and out in short, rapid breaths. As his hands relaxed, he placed his palm against his chest to calm himself, but it felt like a giant boulder pressed down on it.

Knut entered. "The men are confused, Titus. Why must we leave so soon?"

Titus held up a hand. "I need a minute. I'm not feeling well."

"What is it?"

Titus shook his head, but he didn't speak.

"Your plan was brilliant," Knut said. "There's nothing to fear right now. Let the men enjoy a night with extra food in their belly."

Titus hung his head. "What we've done… it will elicit a response. Marmaduke's going to come. We can't stay here. We don't have the manpower to fight. We can't…," his voice trailed off.

Knut waited for Titus to speak further, but he didn't. "You don't know what to do." His voice was measured and matter of fact.

Titus refused to make eye contact. He didn't want Knut to see the fear in them. The old man, standing before Knut, was a shadow of the warrior he once was. Moreover, the legend of Titus was nothing more than a myth. That figure had been built up into a savior who could conquer any army. The men outside had fallen for the lie before, and it ended with a disaster at Kent. Their faith was rekindled by a string of inconsequential victories, that only postponed the inevitable. Marmaduke's army would come, and if they fought, it would be a massacre.

———

DAYS EARLIER, men had clamored to leave the castle, but when the reality hit that they'd no longer have a roof over their head and they'd be exposed to the brutal cold, their eagerness vanished. They still obeyed Titus's order and loaded up wagons and carts. The men took several breaks in between, hoping that Titus might change his mind. Many thought Marmaduke would need a week to recall the farmers and prep the army.

They were wrong.

Two days after the caravan attack, a rider charged down the path and sped through the clearing. "They're coming!"

Everyone gathered around the scout as he dismounted in the bailey. The man gasped for breath, struggling to speak.

"Calm down," Titus said. "What did you see?"

"Marmaduke's army… is coming. They're pulling the logs off the trail."

Knut eyed Titus. This was it, just as Titus had feared.

"How big of a force?" Titus asked.

"It must be all of them?"

It didn't matter if Marmaduke brought half his troops or all of them; they still needed to evacuate, but a full scale assault meant he wasn't coming to lay siege. He was coming for blood.

"They'll be here within the hour," the scout said.

As the urgency of the situation registered, the men stared at Titus. They weren't fully packed. He didn't hesitate. "We leave in five minutes. Grab everything essential and we go!"

Once he'd made the order, there was a release of pressure. The entire group sprang into action, including the blacksmith, cooks, and servants. People threw belongings into makeshift bags. With too much to carry, individuals loaded up the horses, which meant everyone would be on foot. As the minutes ticked away, Titus knew that if Marmaduke's army got close enough, they'd be followed and potentially overtaken.

"We leave now," Titus shouted.

The caravan of wagons, steeds, and men left the castle and flooded onto the north trail. Despite the heavy loads people carried, Titus forced a quick march, the fear and nerves propelling them forward. Any noise from the rear triggered individuals to turn around, afraid they'd see a horde of blood-thirsty soldiers barreling down on them. After an hour, fatigue set in and the pace slowed.

Michael walked beside Titus with a pack slung over his shoulders. "Where are we going?" he asked.

Titus shook his head, unsure. Almost a month of winter

remained. Marmaduke would likely keep his forces at Fennel-worth and send out scouts to search for their army. Since they were weighed down with all the supplies, it wouldn't take long to find them. Once they were found, Marmaduke could either deploy groups of archers and ambush them or he could try to engage and end the war. Regardless, the main trail would be unsafe. "Find Horace for me," he said.

Michael did as instructed and returned with Horace.

"You grew up in these parts, yes?"

"I did indeed."

"Can we survive in the forest?"

"We cannot," Horace said. "At least not all of us."

"Why?"

"Not enough food."

Titus considered his options. "Any villages near here?"

Horace nodded and, in a quarter of a mile, they took a smaller trail northwest to a small hamlet of about fifty people. Titus rode into the village first and assured the elders they wouldn't be harmed. After explaining their plight, Titus negoti-ated for their surplus food. He could've taken all of it if he wanted. It's what most armies would've done, but he paid a generous price with some of Marmaduke's gold and silver.

The hungry men doled out a share of the provisions but rationed the rest. They pitched tents and spent that night in the village's center, another unusual move as soldiers often forced themselves into homes. In the morning, Titus shook the elders' hands and thanked them for their help. He then led the group deep into the woods to a secluded spot. There was no trail, which would make it difficult for a large force to ambush them. The trees prevented cavalry lines from forming, so it was as safe as they could expect, but it was also frigid.

They built three fires and huddled around them for warmth. Isolated in the forest's vastness revealed just how small their army was. Even worse, Titus still had no plan to defeat Marmaduke's superior forces. All he could do was keep the men alive one day at a time.

After resting for two days, Walter spotted an enemy scout in the distance. Knut and four other knights tried to capture him, but the man fled. It was time to move.

The nomadic army gathered their things and pushed north until they found a second village. Like the prior one, Titus negotiated and paid for provisions. And like before, they didn't overstay their welcome. They ventured deeper into the forest and settled into another isolated area.

This time, Titus positioned scouts a half mile south. It remained quiet until the second day when the scouts returned with a group of ten women, half of whom cradled infants.

The lead scout led the cowering women to Titus.

"What happened?" Titus asked.

"These people are from the first hamlet we visited," the scout said. "Marmaduke's men came. When they discovered the money we'd given them, they slaughtered most of the people. He spared the women and children, so if another village took them in, they'd be warned not to help us. If they found us, we'd have more mouths to feed."

"Horace," Titus called out.

Horace stepped forward.

"Take three men and warn the other village. Tell them to hide the money we gave them."

Horace nodded, pointed to a trio of archers, and hurried to the horses.

Titus waved over some men. "Help these people. Get them settled." He nodded apologetically to the women, and they were escorted to the campfire. Titus drifted away to think. *How could Marmaduke do this?*

Titus remembered Charles telling him that sometimes the

victor of a war was the person willing to do what the other wasn't. If Charles was right, then Titus had no chance against Marmaduke.

"We have to stop him."

The voice startled Titus. He whirled around and found Michael staring at him with vengeful eyes. Titus wanted Marmaduke to pay as much as Michael, maybe more, but anger didn't change their reality. "His army is too big."

Michael stepped closer and pointed a finger at Titus. "You promised you'd fight."

Titus gritted his teeth. He would fight, and he was more than willing to die, so long as Marmaduke tasted death first, but he refused to march men into certain annihilation. He hated that his actions had already spurred Marmaduke to murder innocent people.

"We don't fight today," Titus said, and then walked further away into the forest to be alone.

All the marching and sleeping outside in the cold left his body beaten and battered. Every day was a grind just to survive, and his joints ached. Titus sat down on a tree stump to rest, but it didn't last.

Something moved deep within the woods. A man approached from the north. More movement. It wasn't one man. It was many. Titus's heart raced. *Had Marmaduke found them?* He was about to jump to his feet to warn everyone else, but then he spied the long flowing locks of Kensington.

CHAPTER 31

Everyone in the camp stood and mouths hung open in shock. Kensington stumbled through the trees with a ragtag army following him, half of them on horseback.

Horace stepped toward one of the approaching men. "Bedford. It's good to see you, my friend."

The two locked arms and patted each other on the back.

Kensington approached Titus. "You're a hard man to track. Guess that's why you stayed alive."

Titus never liked Kensington, but he couldn't help a small smile from forming in the crooks of his mouth. "Who are your friends?" he asked.

"The Forani. Once they heard Titus had been raised from the dead, they wanted to fight by his side."

Titus arched a skeptical eyebrow. "Is that so?"

"That and they realized Marmaduke would eventually continue north."

"How many?" Titus gestured toward the band of men.

"A little over two hundred."

On average, the Forani were small in stature, but they were a hearty people. The men from the deep north wore thick wool and deerskin clothing, but none of them had armor. Some had short swords sheathed on their hips and all carried short bows with quivers slung over their backs. Those on horses rode with their chins held high—nobles, no doubt. Even the Forani had a class system.

Horace continued greeting many of the Forani. Titus hoped they were as good with the bow as Horace, but even if they were, the odds remained long. Marmaduke still had over a two-to-one advantage.

"Heard about your recapture of the castle and your most recent raid. That was quite nice. Can I have some of that money to pay these men?" Kensington asked.

"Can I have some of your food?"

"Deal."

The leader of the Forani, Odel, was an older man in his late forties. Deep lines from many harsh winters creased his face, and his long gray hair reached down to his shoulders. A nappy charcoal beard extended down to his chest. Despite his age, Odell exuded an aura of health and vigor. He approached Titus and eyed him. "I've heard stories of you."

Titus thought it was a compliment until he added, "I expected you to be more intimidating." Odel didn't say it to be rude. The Forani valued honesty and directness. It may have been why Titus liked Horace so much.

"Stories are often exaggerated," Titus said.

Odel grunted with both agreement and disappointment. "So, what's the plan?"

Titus shook his head, unsure, but Kensington jumped in. "We will raid the villages in the south." He pointed in the direction to drive home his point. "We must force Marmaduke to defend *his* territory. We have speed on our side. The Forani are master horsemen."

Odel nodded in agreement with the assessment.

Titus cocked his head as he considered the implications. "We can't hurt anyone."

Kensington nodded. "Not unless we're attacked, but we will plunder from villages loyal to Marmaduke. We must force him to withdraw to the south. We continue to recruit and build our forces." Kensington didn't leave his plan up for a debate. The king had spoken.

Though relieved not to be in charge anymore, Titus had doubts about this new strategy. How would the Forani know who was loyal to Marmaduke? Many were forced to follow him. Would they be harmed? It seemed as though people would be punished regardless of which side they followed.

AT FIRST LIGHT, a group of thirty Forani horsemen left. They were commanded by Odel, who had them avoid the main roads and travel through the forest. Everyone else remained at the camp and kept a watchful eye for any of Marmaduke's spies.

When the Forani returned, Odel rode in front of the raiding party with his head held high. The troops behind him lifted bags of food.

Hungry men leapt to their feet and cheered. They grabbed the pouches and inspected the bounty. Oats, vegetables, and salted meat were all plundered.

"Any casualties?" Kensington asked.

"A few minor injuries. Nothing more," Odel said.

Titus stepped forward. "Did you run into any of Marmaduke's soldiers?"

"A few villagers tried to fight. We took care of them."

The euphemism didn't sit well with Titus, who walked away without indulging in the spoils. This sort of thing was the reason Titus and Charles's relationship had fractured. Before the last battle and in the subsequent year, Charles had waged a brutal campaign, punishing baron loyalists. Titus had initially rationalized the strategy as necessary, but the list of enemies was never-ending. Over time, it seemed like an excuse to keep people in line. Better to snuff out a small flame rather than risk it becoming an inferno. At least, that was the argument.

As the punishments continued, Titus began to worry that Charles had become the fourth wicked baron, which prompted him to retire from the king's court for good. Charles had attempted to entice him back with titles and lands, recognizing the benefits of having the "legendary Titus" as an ally because when the tales were told, Titus always represented good who vanquished evil. Unfortunately, it wasn't as clear to Titus. Everything had become gray, polluted by politics and greed. After declining Charle's offer, Titus gave an oath never to take up arms against the king. He would never break his word, so Charles had allowed him to leave.

If Kensington now won, what would happen to all the southern villagers? People like Rosalind? Her home was in the south, and she'd already risked her life in a war she'd not asked to be a part of. Titus sat by himself pondering this new dilemma while the Forani laughed and traded stories about the raid.

Michael came over beside him. "Why aren't you by the fire where it's warm?"

"I'm okay here."

Michael was about to leave, but Titus called out. "Michael."

The young man turned. As much as Titus had tried to avoid any comparison to his son, the task proved impossible. He worried about the boy, like a father, but it went beyond that. Even though Titus refused to admit it, he enjoyed having him around. As Michael stood in front of him, he wasn't sure what to say. He simply wanted his company. "What will you do after the war?" he asked.

Michael stared, bewildered, as if Titus had spoken in a foreign language.

Titus clarified the question. "Will you go back to your village?"

Michael looked away. "Will you go back to your home?"

The boy knew how to make a point. Titus couldn't imagine ever returning to his homestead, and before he could respond, one of Kensington's scouts charged into the camp. The soldier dismounted, with his chest heaving. Something was wrong.

CHAPTER 32

The group crowded around the scout on edge, with Kensington in front. Titus remained on the fringe, but within earshot. Everyone feared the same thing. Marmaduke had somehow found them and was coming.

"Is Marmaduke on his way?" Kensington asked.

The soldier shook his head. "He stopped looking for us."

Kensington arched an eyebrow in surprise. This was excellent news, but the soldier's solemn eyes told otherwise.

"He's going to burn all the northern villages one-by-one unless we meet him on the plain of Hattin in two days."

"How do you know this?" Kensington asked.

"I came across a survivor from Lankirk. He murdered the men and left the women and children to wander the forest. They were all instructed to deliver the message to whoever found them."

A hush fell upon the camp.

Kensington called out, "Men, this only proves Marmaduke's barbarity. We must not be lured into his trap." He shook his head for emphasis. "We will continue to challenge his territory in the south until he's forced to retreat."

Some nodded, but without conviction. Others appeared pale or green. Many of them came from villages in the north. They had family and friends in those villages. *Was Kensington really going to let them all die?* No one knew how they could win or stop Marmaduke's reign of terror, but that's why they had a king. He was supposed to have the answers.

The moment was too much for Kensington. He retreated to the other side of the camp, which had become the area where the nobles congregated. Titus followed him.

Kensington didn't turn around and waved Titus away. "I'd like to be alone, Titus." He continued past the camp to a thicket of bushes.

Titus remained on his heels. "We must fight him," he said, out of earshot of the others.

Kensington shook his head, but refused to face Titus. "We're not ready, and you know that's the truth."

"We can't plunder the south while he destroys the north."

"Yes, but the plain of Hattin?" Kensington's voice raised with frustration, but then he lowered it so the men didn't hear. "It's nothing but a giant open field. There's no opportunity for an ambush or some surprise strategy."

"I know. The river also backs one side, so there's only one way to retreat."

Kensington began pacing back and forth. "Marmaduke has over a thousand troops."

"We have the Forani now," Titus said.

Kensington chuckled under his breath. "You've seen them. They have no armor."

"We have to fight."

Kensington stared at Titus with the scared look he'd become all too familiar with. "I don't know how we can beat them."

In the past, Titus would've passed judgment on Kensington. He would've viewed him as a coward, but Titus had been in the king's shoes only days before facing the same impossible decisions. The weight of the responsibility was crushing. It wasn't that their own lives were at stake. It's that everyone else's were, too. "I don't know how to beat them either," Titus said. "But if we die, at least we die fighting." There was no bravado in his voice and even though he couched the statement as an 'if', Titus knew it was all but a certainty for himself, especially when he added, "I will lead the first charge."

Kensington didn't move for what seemed like an eternity until he offered the smallest of nods. The offer had been accepted. They would fight.

For the rest of the evening, the two men talked through the long odds and came up with a plan that neither man felt confident in. Marmaduke had almost every advantage. He had a thousand troops, maybe more, to their four hundred and thirty-two. He also had four times as many knights, but the biggest disparity was the infantry, where he carried a seven fold edge.

The width of the Hattin plain prevented any forces from sneaking up so the formation going in would reveal the attack strategy. Marmaduke would likely march out his infantry as he'd done before, and they'd be equipped with massive shields to stop any barrage of arrows. Once the distance closed enough, he'd call for a charge. His foot soldiers would dash forward and his knights would speed around the flanks. Kensington's bowmen might get a few shots off, but the mass of bodies and steel barreling down would be too much. They'd be routed in seconds.

If Kensington initiated the battle, the enemy archers and crossbowmen would pick off their lightly protected troops. They didn't have the numbers to begin with, and whoever survived the arrows would be swarmed by the infantry. In every case, there seemed to be little they could do to change the almost certain outcome. But they still had to fight.

When morning broke, they sent word to Marmaduke that they would meet at the plain of Hattin the following day. There was a quiet in the camp for the rest of the afternoon as men wrestled with their mortality. Some distracted themselves by sharpening their blades or tightening their bows. A large contingent was tasked with creating wooden spears. When night fell, Kensington ordered another unit to sneak out and lay three rows of logs along the river bank next to the Hattin plain.

Hardly anyone was able to sleep that night. Titus walked the site and did his best to rally the troops, but when they questioned him about their chances, he refused to lie. Instead, he simply said, "It will be God's will tomorrow," and while he could accept the idea of his own death, he couldn't lead Michael to his. He'd agreed to fight, and Michael had agreed to live. That was the deal. Titus had to ensure that Michael lived up to his end, so he searched the area to tell him to leave. He could disappear under the cover of night and no one would ever know. He went from one campfire of soldiers to the next, but Michael was nowhere to be found. At first, he panicked, but then a calm washed over him. Michael had fled on his own. The idea of Michael living out his days somewhere else, somewhere safe, made him smile. Someone *would* live. But the grin fell from his face as he considered Marmaduke's evil and all the people he'd hurt. Titus's son remained buried, a casualty of one man's lust for power. That man needed to pay. Somehow, someway, the legend of Titus needed to be real, even if only for a few hours.

As the night wore on, Kensington called Titus over to an isolated spot away from the men. Titus made his way over. Normally, the handsome king maintained a stoic facade, but not on this night. He rubbed his beard and paced with skittish steps. The jarring sight confused Titus.

"What is it, Kensington?"

"Our plan is unlikely to succeed."

"I know," Titus said.

"If our first volleys don't disrupt their lines we have no chance," Kensington said it as if he'd just come to the realization even though the two had discussed in painful detail how the battle had to play out in order for them to win.

"There's no other option," Titus said.

"Lift your right arm over your head."

Titus's jaw tightened. "I'm fighting tomorrow, Kensington."

"You can't lead the charge if you can't lift your arm."

"It's important for the men to see me in front. They can't hesitate. They can't lose heart."

Kensington nodded. "I know, which is why I'm going to lead the charge. You will lead the rest of the knights."

Titus was about to protest further, but Kensington held up his hand to silence him. "It's an order from your king."

Titus nodded in obedience, but it was more out of respect.

THE DAY FOR WAR ARRIVED, and Titus paced throughout the camp to get a read on the men. If eye contact was an indicator of their chances, they had none, as not a single man looked up. They either kept their eyes glued to the ground or buried their heads in prayer.

The ragtag army only had seven full sets of armor and another four incomplete ones. Two soldiers helped Kensington slip on his well crafted metal pieces that covered him from head to toe.

Knut was also fitted with a full suit. Given Titus's role, he only received a half set, which would leave his joints, legs, and face exposed.

Odel huffed as he watched the noble elites disappear inside

a cocoon of steel. Real men didn't need such protection. Such bravado meant only one thing. The Forani leader had never been in a war before.

The four-mile trek to the battlefield began, and most men didn't bother carrying anything other than their shields, if they had one. Hauling pots, pans, and other equipment required a lot of energy, so the morbid logic made sense. If they died, they wouldn't need any earthly possessions, and if they miraculously won, they'd loot Marmaduke's army.

Titus swayed on his horse and when he passed a lower noble, he recognized the animal he was riding. It was Bucktooth, and the nag struggled to keep up. Titus felt for the old beast and couldn't help but wonder if he'd have the same trouble in battle.

The troops crested a rolling hill and passed through a thicket of trees which opened onto the north side of the sprawling plain. Titus recoiled and shook his head. It was even bigger than he remembered. Ten square acres of emptiness, except today it would be full of men fighting to the death.

Within minutes of their arrival, Marmaduke's forces emerged on the southern edge. Like a never ending swarm of ants, Marmaduke's men marched out of the trees. Despite the vastness of the plain, their swords and shields sparkled for all of Kensington's men to see and fear. Even more intimidating were Enok and Gregori. Encased in metal armor, they both sat mounted in front of a large contingent of formidable knights. Beside them, the archery units gripped long bows while the infantry filled in the middle. The crossbowmen lined the outer flanks of the formation.

The imposing sight left every man in Kensington's army shaken. They stared at death with the only question being which one of the fearsome enemy would be their personal grim reaper.

A pitter patter of droplets perked Titus's ears. He turned and found a trickle of urine streaming off Walter's leg and pooling in the dirt by his foot. The poor lad had no idea as he clutched his giant, jeweled sword with trembling hands.

Titus scanned the rival's ranks until his eyes landed on Marmaduke. Covered with the finest armor and sitting atop an enormous white stallion, he projected the aura of the richest kings, but all of it had been bought with blood. This day was likely Titus's last, and Kensington's army might be obliterated. That he could accept, but he couldn't accept Marmaduke still breathing by day's end. If it was his final act on this earth, Titus had to kill the evil sap, which was far easier said than done, as he had no way to reach him. Even in his prime, it wouldn't have been possible, but he had to find a way.

As Kensington positioned his troops, someone shouted. "The enemy approaches."

Heads whirled to the side, but it wasn't the enemy. It was a disheveled band of twenty men on foot armed with short swords, half of them wood. There were only five actual soldiers in the group, and Titus's heart sank when he saw who led them —Michael. Titus dismounted, hurried over, and pulled the boy aside. "Michael, what are you doing here?"

"I traveled all night going from village to village telling people of the battle that the legendary Titus would lead."

The simple farmers gaped in awe at Titus, but they also saw the imposing enemy forces, which caused myth and reality to collide in contrasting images.

"I told them that if they didn't fight, Marmaduke would come to their village and murder everyone, just as he did to mine."

Titus looked at the handful of actual soldiers, no doubt from the original army who'd been in hiding since the battle of Kent. They nodded to Titus, ready for battle.

"You shouldn't have come, Michael."

"I'm fighting," the defiant boy said.

Titus pursed his lips. He didn't have time to argue, but he also didn't have time to integrate the new bodies into the formation. "Stay in the rear guard. Don't engage unless you have no choice." Titus left Michael and took his position in front of his band of twelve mounted knights.

The boy led the group to the edge of the Balger River, a meandering but deep body of water with a wide sloping bank. It's where Kensington's men had strategically placed three rows of logs the night before. Due to the bank's slant, the timbers remained hidden from the opposite side of the field.

Titus kept glancing back at Michael, then at Marmaduke, his jaw tightening. He now needed to destroy Marmaduke *and* protect Michael, but each task alone seemed impossible.

Drum beats echoed from across the plain and enemy infantry advanced in a measured march. The battle had begun!

Marmaduke kept his important and expensive knights back while the cheaper infantry marched deeper into the plain. The horde of foot soldiers stepped closer to goad Kensington's archers to fire and waste their shots. Marmaduke likely assumed Kensington's army had a limited supply of arrows, and he was correct. Prior to the first battle, Kensington had stockpiled huge numbers of the missiles, but that wasn't possible while struggling to survive in the forest. Fortunately, Kensington had expected such a move. "Only a small volley," he ordered.

All the archers raised their bows to the sky to feign a full volley, but only a third released their arrows, which arced high into the heavens.

The infantry lifted their shields and dropped into a shell, just like last time.

"Now!" Kensington spurred his heels into his horse. He led one of four Forani lines of cavalry that charged the field. Each knight that led held a thirty pound wooden spear above their head with one arm and the reins with the other.

The lines attacked from different angles and they charged single file rather than a traditional horizontal formation. As they closed the distance, the enemy foot soldiers braced for impact. Normally, cavalry stampeded through infantry, but Kensington didn't have the numbers or enough armored men for such a maneuver. Instead, when Kensington and the other leads were within fifteen yards, they reared their arms and launched the spears. The combined speed and weight of the lances turned them into giant missiles that smashed through the enemy shields. No man could withstand such force, and the angled runs allowed the horses to peel away and travel parallel while the Forani horsemen shot arrows into the gaps created by the spears. Shrieks of pain rang out and enemy soldiers dropped, creating more spaces.

"Archers," Marmaduke shouted. "Release."

His archers stepped forward and fired in an attempt to pick off the Forani. The arrows whizzed into the air, but most fell short as the speedy horsemen already charged back to the rallying point. After the first wave, only a couple of Marmaduke's arrows had found their mark, while Kensington's attack had inflicted significant damage.

The lead knights were each handed a second spear, and the lines set out to repeat the run. Titus and Kensington had hoped they would get three passes at the infantry before the enemy knights engaged, but Marmaduke quickly adjusted to their tactic. "Attack!" he shouted.

Gregori and Enok waved their swords in the air and rallied the two regiments of a hundred knights. Hooves thundered against the ground as the mass of men and beast stormed the field.

Kensington neared the opposing infantry, heaved the spear,

and then steered away. The Forani followed, shooting into the ranks, but within seconds, Marmaduke's knights were upon them.

"Go wide and split up," Kensington shouted.

Odel yipped with a loud call that his men recognized. They guided their horses in multiple directions, which left Marmaduke's knights confused and unable to engage.

The Forani rode to the plain's edges and disappeared into the forest. Enok's knights pursued a handful to the treeline. "Cowards! Stay and fight."

Gregori zeroed in on the infantry backed against the river. He realigned his men and charged. Even with only half the mounted knights, there were too many for the infantry to hold their position.

Titus grabbed one of the remaining spears and shouted to his small cavalry contingent, "Keep it tight! Do not break." He kicked his heels into the side of his horse and shot off, guiding his unit toward the center of the charging regiment. It was twelve horses against a hundred, but Titus's men rode in a tight "V" formation with Titus at the point, which made it twelve against the six they targeted. Kensington's archers peppered the enemy knights, picking off several, and every time a man went down, the steed dropped back, creating a gap.

Titus wedged the spear under his arm and gripped it like a joust. No turning back. The two forces were going to collide. Gregori's soldiers lost their will and swerved to the side, but Gregori didn't have time to do the same. Titus thrust his spear forward, impaling the giant knight and sending him flying off his horse, dead. Titus's men hacked away as other knights passed by, but most veered wide and then continued charging Kensington's infantry and archers.

The foot soldiers clutched their swords. No one bothered with a shield, as it wouldn't do any good against the horde barreling toward them. The strongest of men couldn't withstand the impact.

The stampede closed in. The men were about to be trampled or cut to pieces.

At the last second, the line in front leaped backward and dove to the ground, tucking themselves against the first row of logs, which exposed a gap as the remaining foot soldiers stood behind the last row of logs further down the river's bank.

The momentum of the charging knights carried them forward, and their horses jumped over the first log, but the second and third ones caused the animals to stumble, sending dozens of foes crashing to the ground. The remaining infantry surged from the river bank, thrusting their blades into the hobbled knights with a pent up fury. The entire unit of a hundred warriors was wiped out in seconds.

The battle plan was working, but they had no more tricks, and Marmaduke's army was still too big. Defeat had simply been delayed. Amid the maelstrom, a strange thought occurred to Titus. He remembered the alpha wolf, the one that had come for his son's body. After he'd killed the menacing beast, the other wolves skittered away.

Titus scanned the plain for Marmaduke. Ten imposing guards surrounded the pot-bellied man. He couldn't defeat that many, but he might be able to barrel through and get one surprise pass.

"Knut," he turned to the big man. "Lead my knights. Defend to the death."

"Where are you going?" Knut asked.

Titus spurred his stallion and shot out like a cannon toward Marmaduke. As he sped across the outside of the plain, Enok gathered his knights and reformed a line. They wouldn't make the same mistake as Gregori's knights and attacked from an angle. The enemy infantry also rallied and marched toward Kensington's troops.

Titus glanced behind him. The two-pronged assault would leave the men wedged in with the river at their backs.

Walter shouted to the infantry, his voice cracking, "Three lines deep."

It was a true last stand, as they had nowhere to flee and no other schemes. Michael and the farmers clustered together and prepared to fight. Knut led the combined group of mounted knights and raced toward Enok's forces.

Titus tried to refocus his energy on Marmaduke, but something inside wouldn't let him. His grip on the reins loosened, and he no longer urged his stallion forward. The animal slowed and then stopped in the middle of the plain.

Time stood still.

He might be able to breach the wall of guards and kill Marmaduke, but even if he did, the rest of the enemy army wouldn't know about it in time. But what good could he do in the battle—one man amidst a sea of enemy soldiers? He was damned, no matter his choice.

Titus thought about his son. Then his wife. He'd likely be joining them today. What would be the reason—trying to kill Marmaduke or save others?

His face tightened. Maybe he could still save one. Maybe he could save Michael. He jerked the reins around and kicked his heels into the horse's sides.

The opposing cavalry forces were seconds from colliding with Knut's. The giant knight raised his sword and engaged. Swords clashed, bodies flew, and horses reared in horror. The sides mangled together, with men hacking away at each other.

Titus couldn't help there, so he focused on the opposing infantry about to engage with theirs. He angled his horse and smashed through the rear line, completely blind-siding them and halting their charge. Fueled by fear and nerves, the old legend turned back the clock, swiping and cutting down man after man with his short sword.

Walter and the other men capitalized on the momentum shift and attacked the front line.

Marmaduke's archers and crossbowman moved forward onto the battlefield until they were within range of the melee.

"Fire at will," Marmaduke shouted. He didn't care that the arrows had more chances of hitting his own men than Kensington's. He was determined to annihilate the opposing forces, no matter the cost.

Within seconds, missiles sailed into the sky and then rained down on the combatants. Men who were engaged in hand-to-hand battle suddenly dropped dead as arrows pierced skulls, backs, and other body parts.

An arrow struck the hind leg of Titus's horse, causing it to rear and dump Titus on the ground. An enemy soldier tried to capitalize, but Titus rolled to the side and thrust his sword into the man's gut.

Kensington and the Forani re-emerged from the forest and charged the archers, picking them off as they fired, exposed in the middle of the plain.

Marmaduke's crossbowman turned their attention to them, and each side showed their quality, as many fell.

The battlefield filled with death wails, clanging swords, and carnage. The entire time, Marmaduke remained with his rear guard and watched.

In the clash near the riverbank, Titus took out multiple foes, but as the fighting raged, he struggled to catch his breath. Every time he felled one enemy, two seemed to take their place. A ferocious ax-wielding soldier attacked high and Titus deflected it a split second before it crashed down on his head, but he was slow to recover, and the next swipe grazed his lower leg. Titus grimaced and regrouped before thrusting his blade through the man's belly.

Through the mass of violence, Titus caught sight of Michael near the riverbank. Enemy soldiers had engaged with him and the farmers. They were holding their own for the moment, but danger closed in as Enok, now on foot, chopped down men one-by-one.

Ignoring fatigue, Titus shoved his way through the crowd, avoiding blades and punches, but Enok's wave of destruction was faster. The behemoth swung his war sword and cut one farmer in half, which left him squared off with Michael. The size difference would've been laughable if it weren't so dire. The boy had no chance, but prepared to defend himself, anyway. Enok swiped down, and Michael jumped back, his feet landing in the river. He sprung forward, caught a gap in Enok's armor, and nicked his arm. This enraged the giant, who swung low to high, slicing Michael from his thigh to his shoulder. The youngster fell backward, splashing in the water with blood pouring out of the gaping wound.

"No!" Titus lashed out with his sword at Enok, who turned and blocked it.

The legend unleashed a ferocious assault that put Enok on his heels and backed him up, but none of the strikes landed. The giant deflected or blocked the swipes with his sword, and each time, it felt like Titus had smashed his blade against a granite rock. He'd never faced someone so strong.

Enok redirected an attack that knocked Titus off balance and then punched him with his free hand.

Titus's head spun and his vision blurred. All he could see was a hulk of menace charging. Enok swung with all his might and it was only by the grace of God that Titus avoided it, but his foot slipped, causing him to tumble on his back in the river's shallows.

Enok's eyes lit up. He was about to kill the legend, perhaps becoming one himself. The giant man gripped his sword with two hands and prepared to thrust it into Titus's chest.

At the last second, a sword came out of nowhere and forced Enok to redirect his blade and deflect the strike. Knut stepped in front of Titus with his weapon at the ready. Titus slithered out of the water as the two big men sized each other up. Enok had several inches and over thirty pounds on Knut. It may have been the first time in Knut's life when he felt small.

Enok sneered, and his eyes flashed with rage. This was a clash of titans, and he was the best. He unleashed a vicious attack that Knut barely deflected and wobbled him. A smirk swept across Enok's face. No one could match his strength. He continued the assault, backing Knut further into the water. It didn't look like it would be much of a battle until Knut swiveled his chest to avoid a sharp thrust and then cracked Enok in the face with a hard punch that dazed the Goliath.

Knut battled back out of the river, but with one sweeping blade strike, Enok found a gap in Knut's armor that opened a wound on his right shoulder. He hunched over in pain. If he didn't act fast, he'd be killed. Knut steadied himself and squared off.

Enok's eyes flared, eager to end the battle.

Knut stepped forward and dipped his left shoulder to feign an attack. Enok took the bait and shifted his legs to prepare for the death blow. With a quick shuffle, Knut kicked Enok's knee, knocking him off balance, and then spun with a hard sword strike. The giant barely blocked it, but the force sent him splashing into the water and onto his back. Before he had time to react, Knut spun again and thrust the sword down into his chest. The giant man jolted as the blade pierced his heart, and blood pooled around his massive dead body.

The entire duel was over in seconds and, for the first time in a battle, Titus sat stunned. Knut glanced over at him, surprised to still be alive. That made two of them, and Titus nodded in gratitude.

Both men regrouped, and the battle raged on, but it had turned. Perhaps the death of Enok changed it as Kensington's forces had gained the upper hand. Kensington himself remained mounted on his horse and rode along the rear of Marmaduke's infantry line, cutting down the enemy, his hair flowing in the breeze under his helmet.

The Forani had taken many casualties from the archers and crossbowmen, but their superior skill had inflicted more. The remaining bowmen retreated to the forest despite Marmaduke's shouts for them to go back and fight.

The infantry battle no longer raged on the river's edge as Marmaduke's forces had been pushed back, with the horde of clashing steel now in the plain's center. A blood-curdling scream from an impaled foe was the last straw. The spirit of Marmaduke's army broke and men turned and fled.

Kensington and Odel organized a group of cavalry to finish Marmaduke and his rear guard, but the tubby general turned his horse and led his remaining troops in a full retreat.

Kensington's army had done the impossible. Victory was theirs.

CHAPTER 33

Kensington's men shouted in triumph. They'd won, but it had not come without significant cost. Mangled bodies lay strewn across the field, and the ground, once a light brown, now had portions stained red from spilled blood. Titus had fought the enemy to the other side of the plain until they retreated and disappeared into the forest. When the surge of fighting energy faded, it left Titus drained, and he drifted back in a daze. As he neared the troops, the dissonance of the carnage and wild cheering overwhelmed his senses, paralyzing him. Soldiers hugged each other while blood dripped off their swords. Some of the bodies on the ground moved ever so slightly. A hand twitched. A neck lolled. Or a wheeze filled the lungs in a final gasp of life.

A handful of farmers huddled around someone lying in the dirt, which snapped Titus out of his stupor. It was Michael. He rushed over and found the boy lying on his back with his shirt ripped open. The gash from Enok's sword ran diagonally across his torso with blood oozing out and covering every inch of his exposed skin. Michael's chest heaved up and down in mortal panic.

A lump formed in Titus's throat. He knelt down and inspected the wound. It was long and gory, but it had struck no organs. Titus clung to that idea that he might survive while knowing the poor odds. The boy had lost so much blood, and an exposed injury of that size would almost certainly become infected.

Michael locked eyes with Titus. "Did we win?"

"Yes." Titus patted his shoulder. "You did good."

A peaceful smile filled the crooks of Michael's mouth. His eyes closed, and his breathing slowed. He was slipping away.

Titus shook the boy. "No."

Michael's eyes slid open. "It's okay. We won."

Titus choked down his emotions. "No," he said with more emphasis. "You promised."

Michael nodded, but both knew survival wasn't within his control anymore.

"Wrap the wounds. Stop the bleeding," Titus said to the farmers.

Odel rode his horse back from the other side of the plain with a barrel wedged in front of him. "Look at this," he said, while patting the keg. "Marmaduke was so confident in a victory, he brought drink to celebrate."

The uninjured soldiers cheered as they lifted the barrel up and drank straight from the spigot. They didn't bother searching for cups until other Forani returned with more barrels and wooden mugs. Marmaduke had expected his coronation, but the victory now belonged to Kensington and his men.

For Titus, it was anything but a victory. Too many had died and Michael was on the verge of joining them. Titus drifted to the edge of the plain, eased himself to the ground, and leaned against a tree. His knees never felt so old, and a debilitating depression left him unable to move. His eyes locked on a half-naked body on the battlefield. Flies buzzed around the corpse and the hundreds of others littering the field. The sight made Titus ill, and the one man most responsible for all of it still breathed.

Kensington rallied riders to visit nearby villages to deliver the message of Marmaduke's defeat, while the survivors collected valuables from the dead. Despite the morbid task of stripping bodies of treasures, this was a joyous time—the proverbial spoils of war. The living smiled and laughed as they piled up swords, armor, and anything from the pockets of the slain. The nobles would distribute the haul after the giant celebration that had already begun as men chugged ale, danced, sang, and nursed their wounds.

A knight on horseback raced across the plain to Kensington, who was surrounded by nobles already positioning themselves for titles and lands. Knut was among them. He stood on the king's right with his chest puffed out and a full cup in hand. The knight had tracked the retreating army to make sure they didn't regroup for a counterattack. The dancing and cheering quieted down.

Kensington stepped forward and spoke in a dramatic, king-like tone. "What news do you bring?"

"Marmaduke's forces are in full retreat to Doldren Castle."

Boisterous shouts erupted, but Titus remained planted against the tree. The victory party resumed, and the alcohol soon took over as men sang various songs, all off key. Spontaneous chants interrupted many of the tunes. At one point, the men pumped their fists in the air while shouting, "Hail to the king! Hail to the king! Hail to the king!"

Kensington delighted in the attention, but he waved them quiet. "What about our hero who returned from the dead? Titus!" He searched the faces, looking for the legend.

The soldiers shouted, "Hail to the legend! Hail to the legend! Hail to the legend!"

215

The adulation triggered Titus, who jumped to his feet and charged out to the gathering. The group cheered louder as he approached.

"No!" Titus's scolding eyes silenced the group. "Look around." He waved his arms toward the field. "Don't honor me. Remember all of them."

The celebrations stopped and an uncomfortable guilt settled in. Kensington stepped over to Titus. "We will, Titus, but our fallen friends would've wanted us to celebrate. We saved the kingdom from Marmaduke and his oppressive rule." He lifted a cup of ale.

Any man lucky enough to have a mug raised it in support. They needed to drown the horror and revel in the victory. Kensington offered Titus his cup, and the men stared, hoping he would join in.

Kensington continued to hold the cup out for Titus. "How long have we been in fear for our lives?"

The dead still haunted Titus, but he couldn't take away this moment from the men. He took the cup and sipped, which elicited a roar of approval. Titus handed the mug back to Kensington, who smiled.

The king turned to his followers and raised his drink again. "How long have we been in fear for our families' lives?"

More whoops of agreement.

"Now it is Marmaduke who is racing home, afraid for the lives of *his* family," Kensington said.

The men shouted and then chugged their drinks.

The words stopped Titus. "His family?"

"Yes, his wife and son," Kensington said.

Titus froze as he processed the statement. *Marmaduke had a wife and son.* The news fueled Titus's exhausted body, and he charged over to a group of horses tethered to a tree.

Kensington hurried over and caught up to him.

"Titus, what are you doing?"

"I have something I need to finish." He untied his horse.

"Titus?"

Titus stopped for a moment and reconsidered his newfound plan, but he shook off any doubts.

"Titus, where are you going?" the king asked.

Titus mounted the stallion and rode off into the night.

CHAPTER 34

Marmaduke paced in front of Doldren Castle, which was more like a small fort with a palisade perimeter. The castle had been more than safe when he had hundreds of men to defend it, but with a decimated army, it could be surrounded and overrun. Marmaduke hurried throughout the area, ordering soldiers to pack.

He pulled his lieutenant, Tooley, aside and spoke in a quieter tone so no one else could hear. "How many are left?"

Tooley opened his mouth to speak, but he didn't know the answer. Marmaduke's eyes brimmed with fire. Not acceptable. Tooley gulped. "I think we have two, maybe three hundred."

Marmaduke grabbed Tooley by the shirt, who winced, anticipating a beating. The standard practice for bad news. Marmaduke let go and took a deep breath, perhaps sensing his new vulnerability. "We shall regroup at Bainbridge with Lord Gilroy."

The lieutenant swallowed before delivering an additional update. "Lord Chaucer and Lord Gilroy both sent messengers congratulating you on your victory and asking when they will be repaid."

Marmaduke had forgotten that once Kensington had agreed to fight, he'd been so confident of victory, he'd dispatched riders to announce the good news. How would he tell his partners he'd lost?

"We'll press further south to the towns along the sea and find more men. The crown will be ours soon."

Marmaduke's wife, Mitzy, a small woman with dark hair and full cheeks, hurried to her husband. "We must leave tonight. It's not safe."

Marmaduke might have to play nicer with his subordinates, but he refused to cower to his wife. "Woman," he hissed. "I am busy. We depart in the morning."

Mitzy held her hand to her mouth, on the verge of tears and a breakdown. Marmaduke clenched his jaw and his nostrils flared. He glanced around to see if anyone was watching. A marital squabble, especially one over safety, only added to his crumbling authority. He pointed to her and spoke in a slow, cold, and deliberate tone. "Go. Lock yourself in with Paul. You are safe."

Mitzy scurried off, leaving Marmaduke alone. Soldiers raced throughout the camp, but veered away from him when they got near. His grip on the situation was tenuous. Men would consider deserting and there'd be little he could do to stop it if enough of them banded together. He had to project strength. He'd discipline his wife later about her public display. Right now, he needed to focus on protecting his power.

Mitzy dashed out of the shadows, hysterical. "Paul's door is locked. He won't answer."

Marmaduke's eyes narrowed. That wasn't like his eleven-year-old son. He pointed to four soldiers loading barrels onto a carriage. "You, come with me." Marmaduke unsheathed his sword and hurried into the castle. He climbed a small staircase and his heart raced, but less from the exertion and more from fear about the possibility of what lay ahead. Any arrogance and bravado melted as he approached the giant oak door. He pushed, but it didn't budge. The beam had been secured from the inside.

Marmaduke pounded his fist against the door. "Paul! Paul! Open the door."

No sound came from the room.

Marmaduke stepped back and pointed to the men. "Break the door down."

The soldiers lowered their shoulders and tried to ram their way through, but the sturdy wood refused to yield.

"Paul!" Marmaduke's voice cracked and his wife wailed in the hallway behind him. Marmaduke fell with his back against the door and he drooped his head between his knees. How had this happened? How?

Shoes shuffled in the room. Hope. Marmaduke jumped to his feet and stepped away, prepared to fight. The beam creaked as it lifted, and Marmaduke's breath quickened. He gripped his sword, unsure of what to expect.

The door swung open and his son stood there in shock.

His mother pushed her way in front, grabbed him, and held him tight as Marmaduke raced into the room, searching for danger. Nothing, except for the conspicuously wide open wooden shutters. He turned back to his son and pulled him away from Mitzy. "Paul." Marmaduke put his hands on the shoulders of the still traumatized boy and forced him to make eye contact. "What happened? Are you hurt?"

Paul shook his head. "There was a man. He gave me this to give to you." Paul handed his father Titus's dagger. "He said you did something awful."

Marmaduke took the weapon in his hand and stared at it with his mouth hanging open.

"What did you do?" Paul asked.

Marmaduke wanted to speak, but he couldn't.

"What did you do?" his son queried again.

Marmaduke still failed to find an answer.

The boy asked two more times, with the words echoing in Marmaduke's ears.

CHAPTER 35

Under the cover of night, Titus left Doldren Castle. He wandered among the shadows, alternating between doubt and relief that he hadn't exacted his revenge. Half of him still burned with hate, but killing wouldn't have brought his boy back.

The night dragged on and the temperature dropped with each passing minute. A depression nagged at Titus's soul and he feared that if he stopped, it would overtake and suffocate him. *What would he do now?* What was his purpose? Charles was right. He was built for war. It was the only thing he was good at, but there were no more battles, and he was done fighting, anyway.

Titus had heard stories of people who were so cold they had become numb, but they must've been lies because the frost burrowed deep into Titus's bones and tortured him with every step. The black night only furthered his misery, offering nothing but emptiness. His body begged for warmth. For mercy. He would've given anything to feel the way he'd felt during those peaceful nights by the cozy fire with Ariella, when she taught him to read. With her finger trailing across the pages, her soft voice soothed as she spoke, "Humble yourselves, therefore under the mighty hand of God so that at the proper time he may exalt you, casting all your anxieties on him, because he cares for you."

Why had God taken her from him? Why?

Titus drifted through the darkness with nowhere to go. He didn't dare return to Kensington for fear he'd learn Michael had died. Or worse, he'd watch him die from an infection. The hopelessness and fatigue became too much, and he collapsed onto his knees and wept. All the forest's nocturnal creatures fell silent, confused by the wailing human. When Titus couldn't cry anymore, his body curled up and his mind shut down.

He had no idea how long he slept, but when he startled himself awake, it was morning. His eyes took a moment to adjust as a heavy fog filled the forest, leaving everything muted in a soft white, and every breath he exhaled in the freezing air only added to it. Titus shivered as he pulled himself to his feet and stumbled forward. Disoriented, he staggered through the timbers until he came upon a bubbling spring, half frozen over. The twisting body of water triggered something inside of him.

"*Vassar Springs*," he muttered under his breath.

Vassar Springs was where Rosalind had gotten the medicine that saved him. The night she'd left had been one of the worst he'd faced—alone, injured, and dying. The hopelessness he experienced would've broken him if Rosalind hadn't returned. She'd risked her life trekking through the forest at night to save him, of all people—a stranger. When she returned, he'd never felt more relieved and grateful. Even if she hadn't brought the medicine, just her presence and not being alone was enough.

An uncomfortable guilt settled in as his thoughts shifted to Michael. What if the boy was alone and scared while he wallowed in self pity? What if he could save Michael? He had to try, at least.

Infused with a new sense of purpose, he hurried along the water's edge until the village came into view. The medicine woman lived there.

———

Titus left the village and ran with the jar of medicine. Tired, freezing, and still battered from the prior day's fighting, he ignored every physical signal from his body and pushed himself north along the main trail.

When he reached the Hattin plain, Kensington and his men were nowhere to be found. Instead, death's stench blanketed the ground while vultures and ravens picked at the flesh of rotting corpses.

Struggling to catch his breath, Titus walked toward the riverbank. As he passed the scavenger birds, they paused their feasting to caw at him. His steps became slow and hesitant. Would he find Michael among the dead? He glanced at the faces, each one a reminder of the evil that had transpired. His stomach churned as he recognized many of the fallen. Peter Longwood. Nimby Nobs. Garrett from Devonsbrook. And Walter. Titus crossed the entire field and, though relieved Michael was not there, a heavy weight bore down on his conscience. So many had paid the ultimate price.

In the distance, a horse whinnied. Titus turned and fifteen men rode onto the plain, led by Horace. Each horse had a wagon hitched to it. They'd returned to collect their comrades for proper burials.

When Horace caught sight of Titus, he dismounted and walked over. "Titus. I'm glad you are still alive," he said, as if commenting on the weather.

Titus nodded. "How is the boy?"

Horace paused. "Too soon to know."

"Where is he?"

"Fennelworth. Marmaduke's men abandoned it after the battle."

With his head lowered, Titus asked, "Horace, may I borrow your horse?" The humble and almost pleading inquiry caught Horace off guard. The normally jovial man simply slid off his horse and offered the reins.

"Thank you." Titus mounted the steed and rode back to Fennelworth, clutching the medicine the entire way. As he sped across the final clearing toward the castle, the standard of King Kensington blew atop the turret.

Titus galloped through the gate and dismounted in a panic. He was so focused on his goal, he didn't notice the soldiers who greeted him or Kensington talking with a group of nobles across the courtyard. But the king saw him and the urgency in his eyes. "Michael's in the main bedroom," he called out.

Titus dashed inside and up the staircase to the king's chamber. When he reached the door, he froze. What would he find inside? With timid fingers, he nudged the door open.

Men lay sprawled over the floor with various injuries. A healer applied a fresh bandage to a gnarly gash on a man's leg. Titus searched the faces of the sick and dying until he caught sight of the boy sleeping on a makeshift cot along the back wall with a similar wrap across his midsection. Michael's sallow complexion triggered awful memories of Titus's wife and son, which paralyzed his legs. Titus couldn't do it. He couldn't face that kind of death again.

As the healer passed by, Titus grabbed his arm and whispered, "Give this to the boy twice a day." He thrust the jar in the healer's hands. "Make sure it covers all the wound." Titus backed away and disappeared down the stairs.

When Titus reached the bailey, soldiers stopped talking and stared, much like when they first learned he was with them, but the reverence was different this time. It was more human. They knew Titus wasn't some mythical legend. He was a man, like them, but one they respected and trusted.

Titus ignored the gazes and meandered across the courtyard. He didn't know why, but his legs carried him to the chapel. Maybe he wanted to be alone or maybe he had nowhere else to go, but he slipped inside. When the door closed, the room's stillness caught him off guard and caused him to move quietly so as not to disturb the silence. He sat in the last pew and eyed the cross at the front. The bitterness he'd felt the previous time he was in the chapel had gone, surrendered and replaced by humility. Titus wanted to beg for God to heal Michael, but he knew better. Instead, he bowed his head, clasped his hands, and prayed for strength, whether Michael lived or died. He finished the prayer with, "Whatever is Your will. Amen."

Titus soaked in the quiet a moment longer and then left the chapel. Once outside, he took one step toward the main gate and stopped. Where was he going? And what was he going to do? A horse snorted and distracted him. Titus turned toward the stable and found an old nag with a goofy toothed grin sticking its head out the window. "Bucktooth." He approached the gentle animal and rubbed the side of its cheek. The horse nuzzled Titus's hand, begging for more attention, which brought a smile to Titus's face. He'd made a promise to return Bucktooth to Dicun. He also wanted to make sure Rosalind was okay. The idea of the trip comforted him. It gave him something to do. A purpose. At least for a little while.

The booming voice of Knut echoed across the bailey. The big man laughed as other soldiers crowded around him. No doubt, he'd receive the respect he'd craved and lands on top of that. Titus had seen what happened to men when they received money and power. Would Knut fall into the same trap?

Kensington shuffled through the courtyard, giving orders to

the nobles who now looked at him with awe and deference. Would it go to his head? And would he seek retribution on the people of the south?

As Titus took it all in, an inexplicable peace and warmth enveloped him. He eyed Kensington one more time as the wheels turned in his head. *Should he ask?* He walked over. When he was within a few feet, the men around the king fell silent and stepped back.

Kensington nodded. "Titus."

"My lord." Titus stood for an awkward moment while searching for the words. "Rebuilding the kingdom will be difficult."

"Yes, it will."

"If it pleases the king, I would like to serve as your chancellor," Titus said.

The men around Titus shifted uneasily. No doubt some of them had aspirations for such a powerful position. Kensington took several breaths while considering the proposal. The men eyed Titus, then the king, curious what the response would be. Finally, Kensington spoke. "Our kingdom needs more men like you, Titus. I accept your offer."

Titus bowed. Rebuilding the kingdom would be indeed be difficult, perhaps more so than the war, but Titus intended to be a part of all of it. But first, he returned to be by Michael's side.

THANK YOU!

Legend of Titus was a thrill to write even though it wasn't always easy. In fact, Titus may be my favorite character I've created so far. I hope you enjoyed his story. If you did, consider leaving a review on the site where you acquired the book. I love receiving feedback, and it's also tremendously helpful. Being an independent author is challenging to say the least. Every little bit is helpful and your support is very appreciated!

If you're interested in learning more about the story behind this book, please visit https://www.maynardmcnally.com. You can also check out other books and enjoy free short stories.

Thanks for reading!